MW01688781

Christmas Seasonings

A Selection of Short Christmas Stories

by
David S. Gibson
Robert L. Miller
David S. Gibson, Jr.

C.T.R. Publishers
Henderson • Nevada

Christmas Seasonings

©1997 David S. Gibson, Robert L. Miller, David S. Gibson, Jr.

All rights reserved. No part of this book may be used or reproduced in any form or by any means, electronic or mechanical, including photocopying, recording, or by any information storage and retrieval system, without express written permission from the appropriate author: David S. Gibson, Robert L. Miller, or David S. Gibson, Jr.

Cover design by
Norma Harris-Hagan

Interior illustrations by
Norma Harris-Hagan
Charles E. Hagan, Jr.
Mitchell E. Hagan

Limited Edition Printed in the United States of America 1997

ISBN 0-9661692-0-4

C.T.R. Publishing
838 Park Lane
Henderson, Nevada 89015

To our wives,

Christine

Teresa

Rebecca

CONTENTS

Acknowledgment

We express our thanks to Danny Hastings for his creative editorial work, and for his courage in being painfully honest when necessary.

Preface

The stories in this volume were written to illustrate the limitless ways in which our good works may touch the lives of others, especially during the holiday season. Robert, David, and David Jr. hope to make **Christmas Seasonings** a yearly tradition.

For the authors, the joy of Christmases past has been in the telling of stories that flavor the Yule Season with joy, inspiration, and a generous helping of enchantment. It is our desire to share that feeling with you. Our fondest Christmas wish is that this book may enrich your celebration of the season this year and for many years to come.

Merry Christmas

David S. Gibson; Robert L. Miller; David S. Gibson, Jr.

To The Saxophone Man on The Seventh Floor

"Aarrgh! I'm gonna put this stupid thing right through the window!"

Corey Robertson whipped the neck strap off and drew his arm back, tightening his grip on the disobedient saxophone. In frustration, he thrust his arm forward, picturing in his mind's eye what it would be like to really throw his horn. He imagined it flying through the air in slow motion; heard the satisfying crash as it hit the window and shattered the glass outward in a thousand pieces. Cool!

Corey took a deep breath and slowly blew it out. He relaxed his grip on the alto saxophone and stared at it, and then over at his music stand. This new piece of music was giving him fits. Even though the seventeen-year-old had been playing for five years and was really quite good, this was harder than anything he'd ever tackled. He took another breath, ready to try again: but first, something to drink.

Leaving his room, Corey heard a knock at the front door. His mother reached the entry well ahead of him. She opened the door and there stood a black man that neither Corey nor his mother had ever seen before. The man seemed somewhat hesitant and, with a hint of embarrassment, began explaining his reason for being there.

"Hello. My name is Chester Walters. I'm not from around here. I live in Cleveland, but my mother lived on the next floor down. She passed away two days ago and we're trying to get the apartment emptied out before the end of the month. I found this envelope sitting on her dresser. It has your apartment number on it, and is addressed: *To the Saxophone Man on the 7th Floor.* I don't have a clue what it's all about, but is there somebody here who plays the sax?"

"Well, my son does," Mrs. Robertson replied in a rather bewildered tone.

"Then I guess this would probably be for him," the man replied, holding his hand out and offering the envelope to Mrs. Robertson.

"Just a minute. Corey, come here will you."

Corey started toward the front door. He had heard the conversation between his mother and the stranger, and was just as curious about the envelope as they were.

"Corey," his mother asked, "did you know the lady in the apartment just below ours?"

"No, I don't think so."

His mother continued, "She just passed away and this is her son."

Corey and the man nodded at each other.

"Apparently, she left an envelope for you. Do you know what's in it?"

Corey shrugged his shoulders indicating that he didn't.

The stranger, anxious to complete his errand and get on with emptying the sixth floor apartment, stated with a smile, "Well, for whatever reason, she wanted you to have this envelope." He held the envelope out and

Corey took it, thanking him. Mrs. Robertson expressed her sympathy and also thanked him.

Corey returned to the bedroom, his mother at his side, and studied the outside of the envelope. It read:

Apt. 730A
To the Saxophone Man on the 7th floor

Opening it, he removed the sheets of paper. The letter, written in blue ink, was neat and easily readable, and yet the lines were a bit shaky. In one corner, the writing had been partially smeared by a tiny water stain. Corey moved his saxophone out of the way, sat on the edge of his bed and began reading:

To the Saxophone Man on the 7th floor,

You don't know me, but I live in the apartment right below yours. In fact, I think my bedroom is directly beneath yours. I've lived in this building for sixteen years, but lately I don't get out much. I guess you're wondering why in the world I would be writing to you. Well, I'll tell you why.

It's about your horn. Your alto saxophone, to be exact. My husband, Herbert, died seven years ago. We were the best of friends, and now that he's gone, loneliness seems to be my only companion. My children all live out of town, and visitors are few and far between.

Herbert was a musician and played several instruments, but his absolute favor-

ite, his first love, was the alto saxophone. He could make such sweet music. I loved listening to him play. Never did get tired of hearing the sound of that horn. Music was such a big part of his life, and such a big part of his personality. Missing him is missing his music, and I do miss him so very much.

You wouldn't believe what a delight it was for me some five years ago when I began hearing the sounds of an alto saxophone coming from somewhere upstairs. It wasn't long before I figured out that the playing was coming from the apartment directly above mine. And then the sounds of footsteps above the ceiling and voices through an open window revealed that your bedroom was right above my bedroom. The sounds also told me that you were a boy maybe eleven or twelve years old when the playing started.

Corey raised his eyes from the page and thought for a moment. He had been in the seventh grade when he took a beginning band class, and that would have made him twelve years old. He continued reading.

In the late afternoon, which was when your mother made you practice, I would close my eyes and pretend that it was my Herbert that I was listening to. Now, sometimes that was quite a stretch of the imagi-

nation, especially during the first year. The music wasn't so good. In fact, sometimes it was down right painful. But I loved it anyway. Just to hear that horn was a comfort.

You know, this old building doesn't hide sounds very well, and sometimes people hear more than they're supposed to. There were times when I could hear you grumbling about having to practice. You got pretty creative hollering about what you wished you could do with that old saxophone. Your mother would gently encourage you, and then she would not so gently encourage you. And then I remember when the gloves came off, and she would resort to plain old threats. At those times, you don't know how much I was hoping that you were an obedient child, that you wouldn't dig your heels in, get too rebellious and quit. Even if it didn't seem important to you, I really needed your music. There would be a long silence, sometimes for a few hours, and then the sound would start again. No matter how that horn squeaked and squawked, it was music to my ears.

Corey laid back on his pillow, remembering all of the excuses he had used to avoid practicing or to dodge his weekly lessons: sore throat, chapped lips, horn wasn't working right, too much spit in the spit valve, broken reeds, lost music, the neck strap hurt, too much homework, the band teacher told them to rest for a week.

And then he remembered the time that he had traded his saxophone to Kyle Lewis for a computer game. When his parents found out, they went nuts. He recalled having to go back to Kyle and unravel the trade. Corey reflected that partly through coercion and partly through desire, he had hung in there, and little by little the sound had come together. Now, for the first time, he realized that he hadn't been alone in this whole process.

I remember when you were learning one particular piece. The sixteenth notes were giving you fits, and altisimo G took about three months to master. With each failed attempt, I was down here encouraging you. Sometimes I'd be talking right out loud to you: "Come on, don't give up. Try it again. Keep trying. You'll get it." And you did keep on trying, and you mastered each and every one of those trouble spots. More than once, in fact quite frequently, I've included you in my prayers, asking the Lord to bless you and to encourage you in your playing. Even though you don't know it, you've sort of become family.

Little by little, the rough spots smoothed out, and this last six months your saxophone has been just as sweet as could be. I was so thrilled when you started doing some jazz improvisations. That really made me feel close to my Herbert.

But the greatest treat of all came today, Christmas Day, when you played

"Blue Autumn." That was one of Herbert's favorite pieces. I could hardly believe my ears when I heard it. With all my family out of town, there wasn't anything very merry about this Christmas, until that wonderful music started. I just knew I couldn't go to bed without letting you know how much you meant to me. So I'm sitting here this Christmas night writing this note. I've been feeling weaker and weaker these past few days, so I'm not sure how I'll get this to you. But for now, the important thing is to get it written down — the least I could do for someone who has given me so much.

With a grateful heart,
Celesta Walters

P.S. This is probably a little silly, and won't have much meaning for you, but I'm enclosing a photograph of my Herbert with this letter. It's precious to me, and for some reason it just seems right to share it with you.

Corey looked inside the envelope again and pulled out a small black and white photo of a man standing tall and straight, dressed in a suit and holding a saxophone. He had a smile on his face and it looked as if he might have been laughing just a little. Corey passed the picture to his mother.

No sooner had she taken the picture than she gasped, exclaiming "I don't believe this. It can't be!"

The shocked look on his mother's face scared Corey.

"What's the matter Mom? What are you talking about?"

Mrs. Robertson didn't answer, but continued to stare at the photograph. Corey noted that she was breathing harder than usual, and it was as if she didn't hear him ask again and again what was wrong. Finally, taking in a long, shaky breath, Mrs. Robertson looked at her son and tapping her finger on the picture, whispered, "This is the man who probably saved my life — and yours too."

Pulling her son close to her, and with an arm around his shoulder, she told him a story that Corey had never heard before.

"Your father and I lived in an apartment building three blocks from here, and I was four months pregnant with you. It was during the winter, when the days were short. In fact, it was right before Christmas. I had been doing some Christmas shopping. It was starting to get dark, but I wanted to get our laundry done too. We didn't have a washer or dryer then, so we had to use the laundromat. I thought about putting it off for a day but decided that I would just hurry and get it done. When I got to the laundromat, there was no one there but an elderly black man playing the saxophone while his clothes dried . . . . "

❄ ❄ ❄

Christine Robertson opened the laundromat door and was startled to hear the hum and rattle of washers and dryers muted by the clear, sharp tones of a saxophone. She smiled to herself, thinking what a drudgery doing the laundry was, and how this old guy had found a way to really enjoy himself as he went about this routine chore. He seemed to be oblivious to the world and having a wonderful time. The music was quite good, and she welcomed this novel diversion.

Christine got the washing machine started and sat watching the man's reflection on the inside front window of the laundromat. His music had a definite character to it, and she wondered how closely it reflected his own personality.

The machine finally went silent, and just as she was moving her clothes into a dryer, three teenagers pushed through the front door. They were loud and boisterous, yelling at each other though only a few feet apart, and taunting each other with mock fist fights and karate kicks. Obviously, they were not here to do their laundry. The conversation was mostly profanity, and their purpose soon became clear as they went from machine to machine, slamming their fists on the coin boxes to try to dislodge a few quarters.

The saxophone man calmly watched them and moved closer to Christine. He spoke in a low voice:

"I know you don't know me, but it might be a good idea for me to stay close by until your wash is done. Sometimes these kids are just looking for a little money and using up some energy, but there are some who should be taken a little more seriously. They can be mean."

Christine could see that his laundry was finished, noting the stack of folded clothes. She nodded her appreciation. Quietly, she added, "Thank you. Hopefully, they'll leave once they get a little cigarette money."

She was beginning to get a little nervous. The old man walked back over to put his clothes in a plastic bag. As he moved, one of the youths focused in on him. From the other side of the bank of machines, he paralleled the man's movements down the row, walking with almost a stalking motion. Coming around the end of the row, he slowly moved to the old man's side.

Christine tried to watch what was happening without giving an obvious stare. A knot began to grow in her stomach. Her feelings were quickly moving from nervous to scared.

The teenager came up on the man's side where the saxophone case lay open, the horn clearly visible. Before the old man could react, the teen snatched up the horn and was yelling to his companions. Hoisting the shiny saxophone up and down in the air like a newly won trophy, the youth bounced up and down, moving away from the horn's owner. Wiping the mouthpiece with his sleeve as he cast a disgusted look back at the old man, the teen blew on the horn. All he got were toneless rushes of air followed by a short awkward squawk. This brought howls of laughter and a volley of profanity from the other two youths. The first delinquent swore at them. Pulling away sharply from the old man's grab at his sleeve, he blew on the horn again. The result was the same — noisy squawks that didn't resemble anything musical.

Recognizing his failure, the youth became angry. He surveyed the line of dryers and, moving quickly to the only one that was turning, flung it open. He clawed Christine's clothes out onto the floor and threw the instrument inside. Slamming the door shut, he swore at the uselessness of the horn and swore at its owner, glaring angrily at the old man. As the dryer's rotations gained speed, the laundromat filled with the banging and clanking of the brass horn tumbling over and over inside the dryer.

Herbert called the kid a "punk" and tried to push past him to rescue his horn. He first became aware that another member of the trio had moved in behind him when a fist slammed into the small of his back. This was followed by his original tormentor delivering a savage blow to his stomach. The old man crumbled to the ground, fighting for breath. Despite the pain, his head was filled with the destructive clanking of his saxophone inside the spinning dryer. He must get to it before it was totally ruined. But no sooner had he gotten to his feet and begun to try straightening up, than he was shoved and kicked from the side and went down again. Herbert wasn't able to get his hands out in time to break his fall, and his entire collapsing weight drove his left knee mercilessly into the concrete floor. Instantly, he knew that he wouldn't be getting up again. The pain in his knee was agonizing, and an overwhelming nausea totally disabled him. With his eyes clenched tightly shut, he rocked back and forth on the floor, cradling his shattered knee in his hands and moaning. The pain just wouldn't back off.

Opening his eyes, Herbert expected to see the three youths circled around him, poised to launch yet another attack, but he was alone. Turning his head first one way and then the other on the cold floor, he discovered why he had been abandoned. The trio of miscreants was circled all right, but not around him. Instead, they were cornering Christine Robertson. They had her backed into a far corner of the laundromat, away from the ceiling-to-floor windows and behind a row of washing machines. Herbert could see the absolute terror in her eyes and the malicious intent on the faces of the delinquents. Unless something happened quickly, things were going to go extremely badly for the young mother-to-be.

Strengthened by an urgency beyond himself, Herbert blocked out the piercing pain and moved into a sitting position on the floor. Looking out through the store front windows, he saw no source of help. No one was on the sidewalk except a hunched over charity Santa Claus that looked older than he and who was probably so deaf that he couldn't hear the bell he was laboriously ringing. He would never be of any help.

Herbert turned his head and yelled at the three to back off and get away from the woman, but they ignored him. Frantically, Herbert again looked out the window. This time, miraculously, he could see the front end of a police cruiser approaching the corner intersection. If it would only turn right instead of left, they could stop this nightmare. A couple of seconds later, he could tell that the patrol car was going to turn their direction. If only he could get outside. But he couldn't stand, and he would never be able to crawl that far in time. The police car would have already passed.

Herbert thought about yelling, but knew it would do no good. The glass store front would completely block his cries for help. It might as well be a concrete wall. *But it wasn't made of concrete was it?* thought the desperate old man. As quickly as he could move, he crawled to the dryer. Flinching from the pain, he raised up enough to open the door and grab hold of the battered saxophone. Willing all of his strength and energy to focus into this single movement, he hurled the saxophone at the plate glass window. It worked.

The shower of shattering glass was wonderfully noisy. With the windows of their cruiser down, the heads of both policemen snapped around in time to see the explosion of glass and the last bounces of what sort of looked like a completely mangled saxophone. The only one to beat the two policemen into the laundromat was the frail Santa Claus. Skinny or not, he made his presence known. It was amazing how a single blow from a pot of coins could lay someone out cold.

All three of the juveniles, two conscious and one unconscious, were taken into custody. As Herbert Walters was wheeled out to an ambulance, Christine placed the bent and broken saxophone in his arms. The few words she was able to speak didn't begin to express the gratitude she felt toward the saxophone man.

❄ ❄ ❄

As she finished the story, Mrs. Robertson told Corey that she never saw the old man again. From the information included in the letter, his mother calculated that their family had moved into this apartment building sometime after Herbert Walters had died.

Corey asked his mother why she had never spoken

of this before. She explained that although the old man's kindness and bravery would always be treasured, it was impossible to think of him without reliving the terror of that night.

"It was just too hard to think about. Still, there have been so many times when I've wished I could see that man again to more fully express my thanks. And now, it turns out that with your saxophone you've been able to bring comfort and happiness to his wife at a time when he couldn't. I guess that's a pretty good way of saying 'thanks' after all."

After his mother had left his room, Corey looked again at the letter. His attention was drawn to the line that read "*You got pretty creative hollering about what you wished you could do with that old saxophone.*" He thought of the many times that he had ranted, apparently in a voice loud enough that the woman downstairs could hear him, "I wish I could chuck this stupid thing right through the window." Suddenly, he realized how grateful he was that Herbert Walters had done just that very thing, eighteen Christmases ago.

The next night, as Corey went to his room to go to bed, he found lying on his bed a large box wrapped in Christmas paper. There was no tag or card attached, and it was already past Christmas. Not knowing quite what to think, Corey just stared at the mystery box until he heard his mother come to the door. With a slight smile on her face, she easily read her son's confused look.

"This present came a little late. Go ahead and open it."

Still wearing the same confused look, but with a glimmer of excitement added, Corey tore away at the wrapping. Lifting the lid from the box, and parting the folded sheets of tissue paper, he beheld a most unusual sight. In the box lay what was barely recognizable as a saxophone. The side of the bell was caved in, the tube was crushed in one spot and bent along a sharply creased dent in another, the end of the mouthpiece was broken off, and two keys were missing with a third dangling from a bent hinge.

Corey screwed up his face into what had been dubbed by the family as his "crinkled aluminum foil look," and turned to his mother. She just stood there with the same smile, staring into his eyes. Suddenly, understanding dawned. Corey's mouth dropped open and he quickly looked back at the mangled horn.

"Is this it?" he asked, in a voice filled with wonder and reverence.

"I'm sure it is," his mother replied. "After I left your room last night, the thought just wouldn't leave me alone to go downstairs to the Walters' old apartment. I knew it would be all locked up, but I still felt like I had to go down. Outside the door were several cartons and boxes of trash and unwanted items that their son had cleaned out of the place. I found this wedged in between two boxes. I remembered how badly bent and broken the old man's horn was when I picked it up off the sidewalk that night. This has to be it."

As Corey lifted the wrecked instrument from the box, it seemed strange to hear his mother say, "Take good care of it." On second thought, it didn't seem strange at all.

Years would pass. Jobs and homes would change. And yet throughout his life, visitors to Corey

Robertson's home would always find a most unusual decorative touch. Prominently displayed on a table, bookcase or lighted niche would be the battered remains of a saxophone, together with a framed letter which began "*To the Saxophone Man on the Seventh Floor . . . .*"

— Robert L. Miller

Herod's Little Brother

The story is well documented. There were shepherds watching their flocks; there were angels singing heavenly music, as was foretold. There was no room in the inn. A short time after the baby was born, there came to King Herod three wise men looking for the new born King of the Jews.

Herod, hearing the story of the birth of the Messiah, asked the wise men to return and tell him where the baby might be found so he, Herod, might also visit the child. As the wise men left the great throne room, Herod was already making plans to find and destroy this child.

Herod was a mean and insecure man. Any kind of rumor sent him doing strange and wicked things to protect his little kingdom. He would not allow such a child to live very long. This type of rumor would not go away easily unless it was stopped immediately.

At dinner, Herod carried on about the rumor of a newborn king and how these peasants in Bethlehem had brought about a serious problem for themselves by daring to believe such a foolish idea as the humble birth of a new King.

"Well, I shall know soon enough where to find this new King. And when I find him, he will be put to death for all to see." Everyone present agreed with Herod except Herod's brother. His wife agreed. His guests agreed. City officials agreed. But the one, young Matthew, didn't agree. He said nothing but listened carefully.

Matthew was a bit of a student of holy writings. He was friends with a boy named Joshua, whose father was considered a spiritual leader of the Jews.

Matthew enjoyed listening to the discussions that went on at Joshua's home. Someone would frequently ask interesting questions about God, or the stars, or the temple at Jerusalem. Matthew was particularly interested in what was said about the unusual signs in the sky of late.

Matthew was also impressed with how Joshua's family lived what they professed to believe. Matthew at first simply watched as Joshua's father led his small family in prayer, but after a while he became familiar with the topics of the prayers, and began to believe in this God of Abraham.

Matthew did not fit in with Joshua's friends at first. After all, he was the little brother of King Herod, an evil man. King Herod was not liked at all by the people. The taxes that he claimed to collect for Rome made him rich, while the simple people went hungry or without any of the comforts Herod had in his own home. But ever since Matthew and Joshua had met at an important feast a few years before, they had become fast friends, and finally, Joshua's other friends had accepted Matthew as well and had even gotten to like the young aristocrat.

When dinner was finished, Matthew was sent to bed. He carefully slipped out of the palace and found his way to Joshua's home. It was late, and he had a difficult time awakening anyone. Finally, Joshua woke up and let Matthew into his house. Whispering, Matthew asked to see Joshua's father.

"Why do you want to see my father?" asked Joshua, a little guarded and seemingly suspicious.

"Something bad is happening, and I must warn him. I believe he knows the whereabouts of your newborn King," said Matthew.

"What do you know about the newborn King?" The voice was not familiar to Matthew. "Who is this boy, Joshua?" The man who spoke was tall and looked very strong.

Matthew replied, "I know only that Joshua's father said the birth would be soon, and that a new star has already appeared in the sky over the city. I know that three Kings from afar were at the palace, and that my brother wants to know where the baby is. I also know that I must speak to Joshua's father at once, or the baby will not live much longer."

The look on the face of the stranger changed from bold to worried. He ordered Matthew, "Wait here."

After the man left, Joshua said, "What is going on?" Although awakened from a deep sleep, he was now fully alert and could tell that his young friend was serious.

"I need to talk to your father," replied Matthew.

"That will not happen." The man had returned. "You are not to be trusted. We know nothing of the birth of any child. And if we did, we would not tell the brother of Herod. Leave here now!"

Matthew looked at his friend. Joshua just shrugged his shoulders as if there was nothing he could do, but as Matthew turned to leave, he looked once more into Joshua's eyes and saw something there that told him he had not seen the last of his young friend this night. Matthew had not walked far when he was grabbed by the arm from the shadows.

Matthew started to cry out, but a large hand suddenly covered his mouth. "Say nothing, and I will let you go." It was the large man from Joshua's home. Joshua was with him. "Joshua says you can be trusted. I think I am making a big mistake, but this is too important. We must take a chance. Come with us. We will take you to Joshua's father."

Joshua said nothing; he just put a friendly hand on Matthew's shoulder, letting him know it was all right. Matthew was surprised where he was taken. The walk from Jerusalem to Bethlehem was not easy, even though he was young and the road was a good one. The journey took most of the night.

The little house they walked to was plain, nothing special. Outside the house stood several poorly dressed men who appeared to be beggars. Upon closer observation, there was something about the men that hinted that they were not beggars at all, but were instead ordinary citizens dressed to look poorer than usual. They were carefully looking around and appeared to be guarding the house.

The door to the house opened, and Joshua's father came out. He walked straight to Matthew, and, taking him carefully by the arm, led him some distance from the house to a shadowed area next to a small cavern in the nearby hillside. "What is your news, Matthew?" he asked.

Matthew replied, "Three strangers came to the palace tonight. They were looking for the baby."

"What do you know about the baby?" asked Joshua's father.

"Only what I heard you tell your family," was Matthew's reply. "I know He is special, and that you said He is the Son of God."

"Do you believe that He is the Son of God?" asked Joshua's father.

Matthew did not hesitate, "I have seen the signs in the sky, and I can see the new star there, as we speak of it. I am young, but I believe."

"I can see that you do," responded Joshua's father. As Matthew turned to look from the star to Joshua's father, he was a little startled to see the three strangers from the palace standing behind Joshua's father.

"This is the young man from the palace. Is the King your father?" One of them asked.

Matthew answered, "No, the king is my brother."

One of the strangers, looking to the other two said, "We were about to return to the palace to report to Herod where he might find the Holy Child when we were told by a heavenly being that someone would come with information for us that would help us decide what we should now do. We believe you are that messenger."

Matthew was careful with what he said. "You must not return to the palace or even to Jerusalem, and you must leave Bethlehem quickly, carefully hiding your trail, or my brother will search you out and force you to tell him the whereabouts of the baby. I am also afraid that the child must be taken away from here soon, or somehow he will be found and probably killed." Matthew turned to leave having delivered his message, worried about the long, lonely walk home.

"Young man, would you like to see the child?" The new voice was unfamiliar, but there was such kindness in it that Matthew turned half expecting to see a familiar face. "I am Joseph. Thank you for coming. I think you should see the child you have helped. Please, if you have the time, come with me."

As the door to the house opened, a warm feeling swept over Matthew. Upon entering the small room, he fell to his knees. Tears of joy welled up in his eyes as he beheld a young woman and the child she held in her arms.

The young mother reached out a kind hand to Matthew, bringing him closer. "We thank you for coming," she said softly. "This is Jesus. Remember him. He will know what you have done for Him and for all of us. Thank you."

As King Herod's little brother walked back to the palace, he did not know how the parents of the child would protect Him, but he knew they would. He did not know, nor could he have imagined, what horrors were about to occur in Bethlehem, or he would have surely warned every one with small children to flee.

Some things he did know. The Messiah was indeed born, the star was a sign, and he knew that he had done a good thing. When Matthew got back home to the palace, he went to his room, laid himself down, and slept better than he had in a very long time.

— David S. Gibson

The Christmas Gift

Christina had left home a few years ago at the age of fifteen. She had been a reckless free spirit throughout her life. When she was a baby, she was constantly into things she had been told not to touch. Countless were the fragile objects she singled out for investigation and ultimately for destruction. Later, in grade-school, Christina was marked for discipline by every teacher with whom she had contact. Her problem was not a lack of intelligence; on the contrary, she was extremely bright, too much so for her own good. She always had a reason for the decisions she made, and whatever consequence she faced had already been calculated into the equation. Constantly at war with her parents, her first years past grade school were tense. She had no sooner entered the "grown-up" realm of high school than she had fallen in with the fast and free crowd and tasted the baser ways of the world. It was not long before she just decided not to come home one night, and no one had heard anything from her for four years.

Jordan remembered her vaguely. He was five when she left. During the last four years, he had seen his parents in seemingly constant pain and brought to the brink of complete hopelessness. He had heard his mother crying many nights and his father consoling her while on the brink of tears himself.

Then one night the phone rang. Jordan knew

something was wrong by the look on his father's face. It had something to do with Christina, Jordan was certain. His father had spoken quietly with his mother, and she had cried. Jordan was packed up and taken to his aunt's house, and his parents had been gone now for a whole day. The phone rang, interrupting his thoughts.

Jordan's aunt answered it. "Hello. John? What's going on? How is she? John, you need to speak to Jordan. I didn't know what to tell him, and I think he's very confused." She waved Jordan over to the phone. "Here he is. I'll see you soon."

Jordan put the receiver to his ear. "Hello. Dad?"

"Hi, son. How are you doing with Aunt Jackie?"

"Oh, I'm fine, I guess. Where are you?"

"We're in the city at the hospital."

"Is Christina there?"

"Yes. Jordan, I am coming to get you, Okay? Your sister is very sick, and I think you should see her."

"When are you coming?"

"I'll be there in an hour or so. It depends on the roads; it snowed last night. I'll see you soon, son. I love you."

"I love you too, Dad." They hung up. Jordan got his things together and waited nervously until his father pulled into Aunt Jackie's driveway. He met his father at the door, and they stepped out into the cold December night. Neither Jordan nor his father said much for the first twenty miles, but then his father broke the silence.

"Jordan, your sister is very sick. She may not live through the night. She has been through a lot these last few years, and she wanted to be sure to see you while she can."

"What's wrong with her, Dad?" Jordan, though he had not seen her for years and could hardly remember her, loved his older sister.

"Well, son, she's been homeless for a little under a year. She hasn't been able to take care of herself very well. Some police officers found her in an alley the other night, nearly frozen."

"Can't the doctors do anything, Dad?"

"It isn't that simple. Your sister made some choices earlier in her life that led to her condition now. Her body has just had too much and can't take any more. She's holding on because she has a favor to ask of you."

"What's that, Dad?" Jordan could not think of anything he could do that his sister could find so important.

"She wants to tell you herself. We're almost there."

Minutes later, they pulled into the hospital parking lot. On the third floor, Jordan's mother was waiting outside the elevator in the lobby. Jordan gave her a hug, and then she led him down the hall to room 314.

Inside the room was a bed, and on the bed was a woman he recognized from her childhood pictures. In Christina's arms was a baby. Jordan walked toward her. Christina looked at him and smiled weakly. "Jordan, do you remember me?" she asked.

"Yes," he answered. "Is that your baby?"

"Uh-huh. Her name is Shelby. Do you want to see? Come a little closer."

Jordan moved closer and looked at the infant. Shelby looked just like the pictures he had seen of Christina as an infant. "Hello, Shelby," he said.

Christina smiled, as if relieved. “Jordan, I am very sick.”

“I know. Dad told me.”

“Did he tell you that I’m dying?”

“He said you were very sick and that you wanted to ask me something.”

“Yes, I do. How would you feel about Mom and Dad bringing Shelby home to live with you?”

“What about you?” Jordan asked, beginning to realize what his sister wanted him to do.

“I don’t think I’ll be able to come home with you, Jordan. I would if I were able. I want you to take care of Shelby. I want you to be her big brother and protect her from the things she shouldn’t do.”

“I will, Christina.” Jordan said, his eyes filling with tears. “Christina, I don’t want you to die. I love you.”

“I love you too, Jordan. I’m sorry I haven’t been there to be your big sister. I’ve made a lot of mistakes. Please remember that I love you. Please tell Shelby how much I love her.”

“I promise.” Jordan’s little heart was full of emotion, and he felt as if it would burst. He laid his head on Christina’s shoulder. “I’ll take care of her.”

Christina let out a sigh, as if an incredible burden had been lifted from her shoulders, a resigning sigh that exhaled the breath of her life, and she passed away.

“Christina? Christina?” Jordan knew his sister could no longer hear him. As if in affirmation, the EKG that had monitored her weakening life let out the monotone, sustained hum of a flatline. “Mom! Dad!” Jordan gently took Shelby from her mother’s arms and walked to the door. "Christina is gone," he cried.

The family huddled together, tears lining their cheeks. Bittersweet feelings and thoughts filled their hearts and minds. They had lost a daughter and a sister only days after she had been returned to them. But they had not lost Shelby. Christina had passed the last of her life force to that child so that she would survive and fill the gap her mother had created in the family.

That night they took Shelby home wrapped in a Christmas blanket — a living, breathing, precious gift, and a physical remembrance of their daughter and sister.

❄ ❄ ❄

"Jordan, tell me about my mother again." It was the Christmas Eve of Jordan's eighteenth year. He turned his head toward the source of the query, a beautiful image of his unforgotten sister.

"Shelby," he began, "your mother was very brave. I loved her very much." Jordan's voice still cracked a little when he told the story he had told a thousand times before. "Shelby, your mother loved you more than life . . . . "

— David S. Gibson, Jr.

Never Again

Glaring headlights. The terrible scream of braking tires. A deafening crash that jolted her to the very bones. Silence.

There had been a lot of silence since the accident, and too many blank spots that she was unable to fill. Her memory just didn't work. The puzzle that made up sixteen years of her life was simply gone, or, at least, was missing too many pieces to make any sense.

Marie woke up in a room at University Medical Center. Her mouth was dry and her head hurt. The two fuzzy images in front of her slowly sharpened. She recognized her parents. Her father recounted that she had been in an auto accident and had lain unconscious for the past four days. Because of internal injuries, she would have to remain in the hospital for at least another three weeks. She didn't remember any of this, nor much else about her life. The doctors were confident that the amnesia would pass, but for now Marie had to get used to having an uncomfortable abundance of empty space in her life.

The days, hours, and minutes in her hospital bed seemed endless. Although she was very weak and slept a lot, there was still hour upon hour of relentless boredom. Marie grew increasingly frustrated with her inability to put her life back together. She felt like there was no one to help her. Other than her parents, no one came to see her.

Then, on her eighth day in the hospital, as she awoke from a pain-filled sleep, the first thing she noticed was the familiar ache in her head. The second thing she noticed was a girl sitting in her room looking at her. The girl had a kind face that seemed precious in comparison to her otherwise simple appearance, not so great complexion, and plain clothes.

"Hi," Marie ventured.

"Hi, Marie. How are you feeling? They told me you probably wouldn't remember who I am. My name is Rachel. We know each other from school, and we're in the same ward at church."

"Rachel? It's so weird. I don't remember you at all. To me, it's like this is the first time I've ever seen you. But we know each other, huh?"

Rachel nodded.

Their first visit was one question after another from that point on. Marie enjoyed the company. It was the first visit she'd had from anyone her own age. The time passed quickly.

As Rachel started toward the door to leave, Marie noticed her hesitate. An unsure look crept over Rachel's face. "Well, I'll see you later, maybe?"

Marie replied, "Will you come and visit me again?"

"You really want me to?" Rachel answered, raising her eyebrows.

"Yes, please!"

The look of insecurity disappeared just as suddenly as it had appeared. With a smile on her face, Rachel assured Marie that she would visit her again, soon.

Thus, the door was opened to many visits between the two girls. During the next two weeks, Rachel could be found in Marie's hospital room every day after school. A genuine love developed between the two girls. They grew closer and closer, coming to know each other better and better. They shared secrets. They talked of hopes, dreams and discouragements. They spoke of deeply spiritual things too.

The Christmas season was in full swing, and Rachel did her best to bring bits of Christmas cheer to her bedridden friend. If everything went well, Marie would be home in time for Christmas. The two girls spoke often of how wonderful that would be. The long hospital stay was made bearable by the hope which Rachel kept burning brightly.

Eventually other visitors came, but none were quite as special as Rachel. Several girls who assured Marie that they had been her closest friends at school visited her one day for about twenty minutes, sang a Christmas carol, and went on their way. That was the last she saw of them.

The long awaited day finally came. Marie was released from the hospital. She spent the rest of that week resting at home. More than ever, she looked forward to Rachel coming by every day after school. Rachel was surprised when Marie told her that she planned to go back to school the following Monday.

"Why? It's the last week of school before Christmas vacation. Nothing much goes on, and you probably should take it easy for a little bit longer. You'd be feeling great by the time school starts again in January."

"Oh!" Marie exclaimed in exasperation. "That's

exactly what my parents keep telling me. But I can't wait to start putting my life back together. Maybe getting back to school is exactly what I need to jog my memory."

"You'd certainly be seeing a lot of kids that you used to know," Rachel added thoughtfully.

"Rachel, you can't imagine how frustrating and scary it is not to remember things. I really want to do everything I can to get this amnesia stuff over with." And with a mock frown, she shook her finger at her friend; "and I've got my hands full just trying to convince my parents without having to argue with you too!"

"Okay," Rachel answered with a repentant grin.

Marie prevailed, convincing her parents that going back to school that Monday would be the best thing for her. The next few days were a whirlwind of seemingly new classes, new teachers, and new friends. There were so many people that acted like they were really close to Marie. She couldn't help but wonder where they had been during the long weeks she had been hospitalized.

And then her thoughts would turn to her one truly stalwart friend, Rachel. But since Marie's return to school, it seemed that Rachel had changed. She hung back and was hesitant in her conversations with Marie, reminding her of the insecurity she had noticed during Rachel's first visit to the hospital. It was almost as if she was afraid to approach Marie when she was with her other friends. She wanted to ask Rachel what was wrong but didn't quite know how.

The opportunity to talk with Rachel about this never arose. The answer came crashing in on Marie in a voice far louder and sharper than she wanted to hear.

It was Thursday night, three days before Christmas, and Marie was attending a Mutual youth group meeting for the second time since her accident. She was excited about the hay ride and caroling that were planned and was enjoying the company of the other "Laurels," as the sixteen- and seventeen-year old girls were known.

Sister Dyer had announced that everyone was to get into carpools, and a group of four girls had invited Marie to ride with them. They were the same girls who had come to see her once in the hospital. As she left the cultural hall inside the church and headed out to the parking lot, she took one last look around to see if she could find Rachel. It amazed Marie that Rachel could be so open and friendly with her, and yet hardly seemed to interact at all with the other girls, either at school or at church. In fact, Marie couldn't recall anytime during the past week of church meetings and school activities when Rachel had ever been included in the group. Marie brushed these thoughts aside as she climbed into Sister Dyer's car. Only the five of them were sharing the seven-passenger van, so there was plenty of room for all. As they started out of the parking lot, Marie saw Rachel back by the chapel doors — alone.

"Hey, wait a minute you guys. Rachel needs a ride. Let's take her with us."

One girl said, "No way, she can go with Sister Thomas."

Another added, "Spread out you guys so it doesn't look like we have enough room."

Marie was shocked! Were these cheerful, friendly

girls really saying these things? What had Rachel possibly done to deserve all of this? She was shaken from her thoughts as yet a third girl declared, "There is no way I'm going to be seen with that loser."

There is no way I'm going to be seen with that loser. There is no way I'm going to be seen with that loser. The words struck to the very center of Marie's soul. An unholy nightmare spilled out into every corner of her thoughts. Her memory was returning, and it wasn't the blessing that she had thought it would be.

"There is no way I'm going to be seen with that loser." Marie remembered now. It was the day after Thanksgiving, and she had made plans with three of her friends to ride together to a church dance that night. Marie would drive. That evening as Marie was walking down the front steps headed toward her car, her mother called after her with the message that her Laurel advisor had phoned and, because of some last minute problems with the refreshments, would be unable to give Rachel a ride to the dance. Would Marie be able to pick her up? Marie's mind had raced, trying desperately to think of an excuse not to have to give the plain one a ride. She told her mother that she already had a car load of girls, and there just wasn't room for anyone else. She thought to herself that it would spoil all of their fun to have Rachel with them on the drive. Now, four weeks later, Marie distinctly remembered that as she pulled out of the driveway she had said to herself, "There is no way I'm going to be seen with that loser."

Marie's memory had returned. She now recalled that there had been no joyous socializing that night nor had there been a dance. At least, for her there hadn't.

The car accident had intervened. But that accident was the least of her troubles right now.

The ugly reality that Marie had previously acted towards Rachel just as the other girls were now acting hit her like a fist. She remembered the countless times when she had made fun of Rachel: her dress, her hair, her awkward manner, the way she just didn't fit in. She remembered how often she had made cruel remarks about Rachel, not caring if she was within earshot. How unthinkably and unforgivably selfish she had been. If Rachel was a loser, it was because the "in crowd" had made her that way.

Marie felt her eyes fill with tears as she questioned how she could ever have treated such a dear and faithful friend as Rachel in such a heartless fashion. But thanks to her car accident, she had been given a second chance. She now had the opportunity to view an instant replay of this pitiful segment of her life and to correct her mistakes.

Marie surprised herself with the words that leaped from her mouth. With a firmness born of a penitent heart, she announced, "This isn't right. We're not going to do this to Rachel anymore. At least, I'm not. Never again." Marie got out of the car and walked over to the chapel doors where Rachel was still waiting. With a tear-stained face she hugged her dear friend and told her of the revelations of the last few moments. Marie was amazed at the gracious smile and nod of acceptance which met her pleas for forgiveness. How could one who had been so wronged be so forgiving?

The two girls sat side by side in Sister Dyer's van that night. From that time forward things began to change. At first, the hesitancy was still there on Rachel's part, but Marie was bound and determined not to have her left out. She had made a mistake once and would never make that mistake again. Marie was not alone in this repentance process. Others followed her lead, discovering that their shallow surface judgments of Rachel had been illfounded. Here, waiting to be discovered, was a warm and caring person with much to offer in the way of friendship.

When the presents beneath that year's Christmas tree had been long forgotten, the friendship born between Marie and Rachel continued to grow. The bittersweet lessons of that Christmas would serve both girls well throughout their lives. These lessons would be forgotten — never again.

— Robert L. Miller

I'll Match It

"I'll tell you what, Kyler, if you save part of your allowance and the money you earn to pay for half of that bike, I'll match it." It was late March, and all of Kyler's friends were learning to ride their bikes without training wheels. They had started going on bike rides, and he had to stay behind because times were tight.

"Okay, Dad. How much do I need to save?" the six-year-old boy asked. He was good at math but had not learned to do division yet in school.

"Well, the bike you want costs $120, so you will need to earn sixty dollars," his dad answered.

"Whoa! That's a lot of money. How can I save that much?"

"Well, you get two dollars every payday from me for allowance. If you save it all, you'll have almost half of the money you need before Christmas."

"Grandma pays me a dollar each week for pulling her weeds too!" The thought of all that money got Kyler excited. He had a special place he kept his money. It was a little, metal pencil-holder with his favorite Star Wars character on it. Right then, it was empty. His mom had taken him to the store to buy his favorite comic-book action-figure, Batman. But now, Kyler was serious. He wanted a bike. Looking up, he stated, "I'm gonna save all my money, Dad!"

Kyler ran excitedly to his room where he kept the pencil can. Picking it up and shaking it, he reaffirmed that it was still empty. He knew he would fill it up soon. Placing the can under his pillow, Kyler picked up his Batman toy and bolted for the door.

"Kyler, is your room clean?" his mom called.

"Yeah, Mom. I'm going to play with Charlie!" he called back, already letting the screen-door go behind him.

Charlie was Kyler's best friend. He lived three houses down the street. They had been in the same pre-school and kindergarten classes, and now they had the same first grade teacher. Inseparable, the two boys never went anywhere fun without each other, except when their parents took them out of town, and even then they could usually find some way to go with each other. To-day, however, something was different. As Kyler came closer to the third house down, he saw Charlie's dad keeping Charlie balanced on a shiny blue bike.

"Hi, Kyler!" Charlie yelled. "Look what my dad got for me!"

Kyler smiled, "Cool bike, Charlie! Can you ride yet?"

"If he'll stop talking long enough, he might get it." Charlie's dad said. "Kyler, why don't you sit down and watch? Charlie needs to learn to ride this bike today while I have time to teach him. So try to be quiet."

The smile slipped from Kyler's face as he slumped to the ground, Indian style. For a long time, he sat there watching Charlie wobble and fall, then wobble and fall again. By the time the sun was low on the horizon, Charlie had gotten it down. "Wow, Charlie! You can really ride a bike!" Kyler congratulated.

"Thanks to my dad." Charlie rejoined with a smile.

"Well, boys. It's getting late. Kyler, you should probably run along home now. You can play with Charlie tomorrow." Charlie's dad said.

"Okay, Mr. Thompson." Kyler mumbled, bowing his head dejectedly. "See ya, Charlie."

"See ya."

❄ ❄ ❄

Early the next morning, Kyler was up and ready. He couldn't wait to go check out Charlie's new bike. Working quickly, Kyler hurried around the house excitedly. "Mom! My chores are done! Can I go play with Charlie?"

"Yes, make sure you come home before lunch. We are going to Grandma's today so you can pull weeds."

"Oh yeah! Great, Mom! I'll be back." At this, he rushed to the door, opened it, and ran as fast as he could to Charlie's house.

On Charlie's porch, the Jones brothers and a few other kids were grouped around Charlie's new bike, all with bikes of their own. They were all wearing jackets despite the summer sun. Charlie came out wearing a jacket too, just as Kyler walked up the driveway.

"Hi, Charlie!" Kyler called. "Wanna play?"

Before Charlie could answer, Jason Jones, a mean boy Kyler's age, took a step forward. "Charlie's in our bike club. We's a club. You ain't a member, so git outta here." Jason met Kyler at the edge of the porch. Jason's face was dirty and so were his fingernails; he had ratty, dirt-brown hair and freckles all over his pudgy, runny nose. "You gotta have a bike to be in our club. And you gotta wear a jacket for pertekchun."

"For pro-tec-tion?" Kyler asked, emphasizing the correct word.

"Yeah, pertekchun. You ain't got 'em, so git outta here." This was said with a push for emphasis.

"I do have 'em!" Kyler said, brushing himself off. "Wait a minute while I go get my bike and jacket."

"Okay, but hurry up." Charlie piped up.

Hurrying home, Kyler rushed into his room, looking for a jacket. All he could find was a hooded sweatshirt. "Mom! Where's my jacket?" He called desperately.

"It's put away with your winter clothes, Kyler. It's summertime, son."

"But I need it, Mom."

"What for?"

"For protection."

Kyler's mom looked at him questioningly. "Why don't you just wear that sweatshirt? It'll do just as well."

"Oh, I guess it'll do," he grumbled.

Now he needed a bike. In his backyard was his old plastic Thunder Wheels three-wheeler bike. Mounting the toy bike, Kyler tore off towards Charlie's house only to see the club starting to leave. Jason looked back and laughed, "Look at the little sissy on his Thunder Wheels! Let's ditch 'im!" All of them, including Charlie, stood up on the pedals and began cranking their wheels furiously, leaving Kyler crying in their dust.

❄ ❄ ❄

"How is my Kyler doing?" Grandma said when they arrived at her house.

"Okay, I guess," he replied.

"Come in and have some lemonade and cookies.

Would you like that?" She saw him nod. "Why are you sad, Kyler?"

"Because my best friend Charlie doesn't want me in his club." Kyler couldn't hold back his tears any more, and moisture filled his eyes anew.

"Well, that's not very nice of him. Don't worry. You don't need to pull weeds today."

"No, Grandma, I have to! Dad said he would match me if I could pay for half of a new bike. I need to save up enough money." Kyler's face had taken on a very worried, anxious look.

"Well then, I guess you had better finish your lemonade and go pull some weeds." Grandma smiled. Kyler gulped down the last of it and hurried outside. He would save his money and get his new bike no matter what.

❄ ❄ ❄

Autumn colors were on the trees outside Kyler's house; he sat listening to the wind and counting the money on his bed. Besides allowance and working for Grandma, Kyler had been industrious around his neighborhood. While the Jones boys and company were riding around as a club, Kyler was earning a quarter per chore from their parents. Altogether, he had already earned forty-eight dollars.

"Hey, I'm almost there!" Kyler thought to himself. "Another month and I'll have my bike." So busy with his personal celebration, Kyler didn't notice the knock on his bedroom door until it came again. "Come in," he said, sliding his refilled pencil can under his pillow.

Charlie entered the room.

"Hi, Kyler," he said. "Do you wanna play?"

"I can't. The club won't let me," he answered.

"Well, um, they won't let me either."

"Why not?"

"Because somebody stole the chrome caps off my tire tubes." Charlie was obviously upset.

"Chrome caps?" Kyler asked, not sure of what he meant.

"Yeah," said Charlie, "they're the coolest. Instead of black rubber caps, these are chrome. They keep the air in your tires. The club steals them off cars all the time, but I already had them on my bike; dad would kill me if I stole some."

"Why doesn't Jason give you some of his?"

"He says I gotta steal my own. I wouldn't, so they kicked me out."

"Oh. Well, you don't need chrome caps to play with me." Kyler smiled forgivingly.

"Thanks. Do you wanna come to my house? My dad says he'll teach you to ride on my bike if you want." Charlie offered.

"Gee, thanks!" Kyler's mood brightened right up, and the two boys headed for Charlie's house just like they had always done before the bike club.

❄ ❄ ❄

It was early December, and Kyler had earned seventy dollars. He couldn't wait to tell his dad. Hurrying down the hall to his parents' room, Kyler stopped abruptly at the sound of his parents' voices. They seemed to be having a very important discussion, and he didn't want to interrupt, no matter how exciting the news was.

"Honey, I don't know what we're going to do about Christmas. My boss said we get a turkey as our Christmas bonus this year instead of an extra check," Dad said.

"What? How can they do that?"

"He said the profits were down company-wide this quarter, and they had to cut back." Kyler could hear the tremor in his dad's voice.

"Well, I guess we can make do. I don't need any presents. We'll be all right with the things we have."

Kyler knew his mom wanted a new set of knives. She was a good cook, and she always said that good sharp knives were the secret. The ones his parents had received as a wedding gift showed years of use.

"And these old work gloves will have to last a few more months." Kyler's dad had been working construction while he waited for word about a position in a firm for which he had applied.

Kyler turned and crept back to his room. He knew that a bike would cost too much for his dad, even though he had half of what was needed already. Kyler realized that no one in his family would get presents this Christmas. Then he had an idea. Going to the kitchen, he picked up the phone and dialed Grandma.

"Hello," came her friendly voice.

"Grandma? This is Kyler."

"Hello, Kyler. How are you?"

"I'm fine. Grandma?"

"Yes, Kyler?"

"Can you take me to the store?"

"Well, sure. I can do that. Why do you want to go to the store?"

"It's a surprise for Mom and Dad."

"Wonderful," said Grandma. "I love surprises. Why don't you hang up so that I can call back and ask your mom if I can come and get you?"

"Good idea, Grandma! I'll hang up now." It was good to have her on his side.

❄❄❄

At the store, Kyler made his Grandma walk a few feet behind him so — he thought — she could not see what he was getting. First, he found a set of knives for his mom. Wanting to do something special, he also found a pretty wall-hanging for her kitchen. For his dad, he found a new pair of leather gloves and also a tie for when he got the job at the firm. He got a new set of chrome caps for Charlie. Then he made Grandma close her eyes while he put an embroidery hoop and a bunch of different colors of thread into the basket.

As Kyler paid for it all, he smiled. He felt nice inside. He had a warm feeling that pushed away the sadness he felt at the thought of not getting the bike for which he had worked so hard.

Grandma could not contain the question any longer. "Kyler, isn't that the money you saved for your bike?"

"Yes, Grandma," he answered.

"What about your bike?"

"I don't think that Dad can afford it. Besides,

Mom and Dad need these things. I heard them talking."

Grandma blinked back tears and smiled, "Well, there's still time to write to Santa. Maybe he can bring you a bike."

Kyler thought about Grandma's proposal all the way home.

❄ ❄ ❄

DEAR SANTA,

MOM AND DAD ARE HAVING A HARD TIME THIS YEAR. I HAVE TRIED TO BE A GOOD BOY, BUT SOMETIMES I AM BAD. PLEASE SANTA, DO YOU THINK YOU COULD BRING ME A BIKE?

IT DOESN'T HAVE TO BE NEW. I LEARNED HOW TO RIDE ON CHARLIE'S BIKE, AND I PROMISE TO TAKE GOOD CARE OF IT.

LOVE,
KYLER

Kyler gave the letter to Grandma because she said she had connections with St. Nick and could make sure he got it in time.

❄ ❄ ❄

Late Christmas Eve, Kyler sneaked out of his

room and placed his gifts under the tree. He couldn't wait to see Mom's and Dad's faces in the morning. Charlie had smiled so much when Kyler gave him the chrome caps, Kyler thought his face would split. Kyler went back to bed, anxious for morning to come.

❄ ❄ ❄

Grandma arrived with her gifts at seven o'clock sharp. Kyler had already been wide awake for two hours. "Merry Christmas, Grandma!" he cried when she opened the door. "Mom! Dad! Grandma's here! Come and open your presents!"

The little family was soon gathered around the little tree. Dad said to Kyler, "Kyler, why don't you look under the tree and pass out the presents to everyone?"

Kyler excitedly bounded toward the tree and came back with the presents for Mom, Dad, and Grandma.

"Oh, Kyler," said Mom, tears filling her eyes. She hugged the boy close and thanked him for the gifts.

"Thank you, son." Dad was smiling. "We love you very much. Go and get that red envelope off the tree. I think Santa left it for you." Kyler had been eyeing that particular envelope anxiously. The adults exchanged happy glances as he rushed to open it.

Examining the contents, awestruck, Kyler read aloud:

Dear Kyler,

Thank you for your letter. You have been a very good boy. You gave up your bike so that your parents could have Christmas. I didn't have any old bikes for good little boys. I did bring something though, and it's too big to go under the tree. Go look on the back porch. Merry Christmas!

Love,

Santa

P.S. Thanks for the cookies.

The back door shut over these last few words as Kyler sprinted for the back porch. There, shining in glory was a metallic-red, sparkling new bike.

— David S. Gibson, Jr.

Joy Nearly Lost

Thinking back over the two years since they lost little Davy-boy, it was hard trying to fill in the blanks. Things just sort of go blank when you lose a child. All the months of blood tests, x-rays, spinal taps, chemical therapies, special diets, quarantines — all of the other special daily arrangements that were required, but which then ended very suddenly left their lives in turmoil, their holidays in shambles. They didn't know how they would ever have another merry Christmas. Probably they wouldn't. Those were the thoughts of a young mother and father on that cold, crisp November morning. That morning, more was about to happen than the biggest shopping day of the year.

"How did you sleep last night?" Jake asked.

Terri heard his question but didn't answer. She really hadn't said much at all in the two years since her child died. There had been a warning, if you wanted to call it that. Davy had been quite ill for about three months. ITP, they had called it: a leukemia-like illness. He was doing better, the doctors had said, and he even looked better. The steroids had made him gain a lot of weight, but the platelet count in his blood was finally rising. Now she thought hard about the warning.

❄ ❄ ❄

"Mommy, Daddy, wake up. I need to tell you

something. Jesus came and visited me last night."

Davy hadn't seemed overly excited; in fact he was as calm and mature-looking as a young adult. She remembered being alarmed that her three-year-old had looked like a young man that morning. What he had said was cute. His blond hair was messed up from the night's sleep, but his big blue eyes were as clear as a summer sky.

"He did, did he? How did you know it was Jesus?" This was amusing.

"I've seen Him before. We have some pictures of Him on the bookshelf, and I have a picture in my room that Grandma Mary gave me." Davy didn't flinch; he talked like it was just an everyday thing. "He's coming back tonight."

"What did He want?" Jake asked.

Jake was suddenly wide awake. Terri felt something vaguely familiar. Something in her chest began to burn, and her throat was all tight. She took Davy into her arms and held him very close.

"Why is He coming back tonight sweetheart?" She began to panic just a little as did Jake, although neither really knew why at the moment.

"Well Mommy, He said I've had enough. I can go with Him tonight if I want to. He took me to my favorite place up on Naples Street and let me look at the whole city."

Davy loved to sit in the car on the top of the hill on Naples street so he could see all around.

"It sounds like you were dreaming son. Come here and give Daddy a big hug."

"I wasn't dreaming, Daddy. He was here. I think

I'll go with Him. I have had enough."

Davy climbed down off of his parents' bed and went back to his room.

"What do you think that was all about? It was kind of . . . well I didn't like that at all." Jake was up now, not really going anywhere, just pacing. "Jesus wouldn't do that would He? At least not without talking to us first. I mean, He ought to have to at least get permission to talk to our little boy. This isn't something Davy is even old enough to understand, let alone decide for himself. The doctor just told us he's doing better. Well, we'll just sleep in his room tonight, and we won't let him go. We'll discuss it with Him first before He takes our little boy . . . What am I saying anyway? He didn't come here; we would have known."

That had been it. That had been the warning. She knew it now as she recalled the burning in her heart, and the tightness in her throat. She remembered her words to Davy-boy before he went to sleep the next night.

"I love you son. I can't be happy without you here. So if Jesus comes tonight you be sure to tell Him Mommy won't let you go. Will you tell Him, Davy?"

When her little boy looked up into her eyes, tears were there. "I love you, Mommy. But I want to go with Jesus. I hurt too much. You'll be all right. I love you too, Daddy. I'm very tired now."

He gave them each a big hug, took hold of his teddy bear, laid down and went to sleep. Terri had stayed awake most of the night, but finally she and Jake had both fallen asleep at the foot of his bed. When they woke up their precious little boy was dead.

❄ ❄ ❄

"Are you ready to go dear?" Jake had the flowers in the car and was putting on his jacket. "We need to hit the road if we are going to do some shopping after."

"Jake . . . I feel so sad this morning. When will we stop feeling so sad?"

"I don't know, Terri. Maybe we won't. I think it's the season and the smells of the holidays. I can hardly stand it. Well, it'll be over soon. Only ten more shopping days 'til Christmas, and it'll be spring before you know it. Come on girl, let's get going." Jake tried hard to hide his heartache. "Christmas, humph, big deal," he said to himself.

It was always hard on them to make the drive up Naples Hill to the cemetery. So many memories were hidden there just waiting to seize them as they drove by Davy's favorite spot. Today was no different. In fact when Terri gasped, Jake figured it was just another memory, until he saw the little boy himself and nearly ran right off the road. Jake stopped the car suddenly. Both of them just stared at the little blond-headed boy. They could tell right away that he was very cold.

"What kind of a mother would let her child out in this cold without a coat? Come on Jake; let's find out what's going on." Terri was out of the car and hurrying toward the little boy. It was nearly a race as Jake stepped quickly behind her.

"Now, be careful, Terri. You don't want to scare him."

To their surprise, the little boy really didn't even notice them. He was looking at a book, and although he shivered, he didn't seem to be concerned with much. Terri just stood there looking at the little boy. Finally Jake reached down and put his hand on the boy's shoulder.

"What are you reading?" The question was a simple one. The reply was too.

"I can't read. I'm only five. But I like to look at the pictures. You know, just in case Santa comes this year, I have to know what me and my mommy want. He didn't come last year, but my mommy thinks he might come this year." The book was a toy catalog.

"Where is your coat? It's pretty cold out here." The wind mussed his blond hair. Not realizing what she was doing, Terri removed her sweater and draped it over the shivering boy's shoulders. "Where do you live?"

"We live in back of a lady's building. She has a little trailer where she lets us stay until we can buy a real house." The small boy seemed unconcerned.

"Where does your daddy work?" Jake didn't want to pry, but he was worried about the boy, and now he knew there was at least a mom somewhere.

"My daddy is dead. He got real sick when I was just a little boy. My mommy told me about it."

"Jake, let's take him home to his mother and see if there's something we can do to help them out." The little boy jumped up and began to walk off.

"I can't go anywhere with strangers." His walk turned into a run, and he was around the corner and out of sight before they had time to react. Jake ran around the corner with Terri right behind him, but the boy had vanished. Terri's sweater lay on the ground.

"Little boy, where are you?" They looked around

for quite a while, but could not find the blond-haired boy anywhere. They walked to the car and got in.

"How will we ever find him, Jake? He's so small and so cold." Terri began to cry softly. Jake put his arm around his wife and pulled her to him. He noticed for the first time in a long time how good her hair smelled. He held her close for quite a long time, and then he started the car.

They drove the short distance to the cemetery in silence. When they arrived, they opened the trunk of the car and removed the small bouquet of flowers, carefully chosen from what remained in the garden after the frost had put most of the bushes to sleep. Terri placed them carefully on the small headstone that marked the grave of their beloved son. The headstone was simple. Pink sandstone from the hills at the Valley of Fire, little Davy's favorite picnic place.

Actually, the Valley of Fire was the only place Davy had ever been for picnics since he had started talking. But he had loved the hikes his mommy and daddy had taken him on. And he had been so taken with the beauty of the red sand and mountains. After Davy died, his daddy had gone for a long drive, and when he got home, he had the large piece of sandstone in the trunk of the car.

The cemetery had argued with them at first, saying that they had some kind of contract with a headstone company. All the headstones had to be purchased through them. Jake had persevered, and the cemetery finally gave in, as long as Jake let their company do the carving. It read:

David Isaac Adams
Born August 23, 1973. Died December 15, 1976.
He agreed to come to earth,
and he agreed to leave with Jesus.
We miss and love him.

Terri liked little lambs, so there were carved three little lambs playing, just below the words.

Both parents just stood there looking at the headstone for a long while. It was always this way. Then little by little conversation would begin, mostly memories of events where Davy had done something cute or clever. Then memories would flood back of times nearly forgotten, spoken of only once each year: the anniversary of Davy's death. Suddenly the conversation steered away from the customary talk about Davy and to the little boy on the top of Naples Hill.

"Did you see how big and blue his eyes were? And how cold he was? He was poor, Jake. He said he didn't get anything from Santa last year."

But Jake's eyes hardened. "Lots of people have it tough at Christmas, Terri. Like people left without their child just before Christmas. He probably doesn't even know the difference. One Christmas is just like another to a kid like that."

Terri looked at him in surprise. "He's just a little boy, Jake. He deserves to be happy!"

"Like Davy deserves to be happy?" Jake wanted the words back, but they were out there, and the damage was done. Terri's eyes filled with tears, pain showed all over her face. Not able to stop himself, he went on.

"What did Davy ever do to deserve all the pain, all

the lost dreams? What did we do to deserve to lose our precious little boy? We go to church. We serve those in need. We tell the truth, give to the needy. We took good care of Davy. And he was a good boy. He was the best. I really don't want to hear about some poor little boy who didn't get anything from Santa Claus. At least he's alive."

It always ended the same. They didn't want it that way, but at some point the anger always seemed to take over, and they would go home in silence, silence that seemed to last until the next visit to the cemetery. A year is too long to go without talking, and they both knew it. But neither of them could do anything. They were powerless against their pain and grief.

As they entered the house, Jake realized they had forgotten again to buy a Christmas tree. He sat down in the big stuffed recliner. Terri sat at his feet, resting her back against his legs. Her head fell back on his lap. He thought about the tree. He could still see it clearly in his mind, and he could still remember the excitement. He didn't notice Terri get up and go to the kitchen.

He remembered Davy's first Christmas that had actually meant something. Jake and Terri had caught Davy a dozen times trying to open presents. He had sat on Santa's lap for the first time that year and asked for a new bike and a Darth Vader Star Wars figure. Both presents and many more still sat on the floor of his room. The name tags still hung from the bike and action figure, and the large pile of presents was still wrapped, waiting to be opened.

That tree had been the best one of their young marriage. Of course it had been their first Christmas out of law school, so they had money to burn compared to their school days. Jake had put hundreds of lights on the tall tree, and, with all the ornaments they had collected together, the tree was a twinkling work of art, just calling to their three-year-old. It had that effect on Jake too.

Christmas had been Jake's favorite time of year before Davy died. He and Davy would lie on the floor with just the tree lights on until Davy fell asleep. Jake would put Davy to bed and then lie there for another half hour until Terri would come and make him go to bed.

As Terri came back from the kitchen, she could hear Jake snoring softly. She went over to the big chair where Jake slept and stood beside him. In her mind she pictured Jake and little Davy asleep in front of a big lighted tree. She touched his hair, leaned down, and kissed his forehead. Kisses while he slept. That had become the norm with only a few exceptions. They argued too much to feel like kissing very often.

"I'm sorry for the way I act these days," she thought. "What has happened to us?"

She then did something which she had been avoiding in the two years since her son died. She knelt down and began to pray. For some reason she needed to believe again. She wanted the comfort believing gave her.

"Please, Heavenly Father, help us to heal." She didn't feel anything different, but she went on. "Please bless the little boy we saw today. We are so fortunate. Please forgive Jake for the things he said. He didn't mean it. We're both confused, and so hurt. Help me to change. Please help Jake to heal. I need my husband back, and I know he needs me back. It's Christmas time. Please let us have the feelings we used to have at this special time of year." She closed her prayer.

Terri gently woke her husband enough to lead him to the bedroom. She had already pulled back the covers. She helped him lie down, and covered him up. As she bent down to kiss him goodnight, he reached up and pulled her to him. He kissed her on the lips.

"I'm sorry for the things I said. I don't want to be bitter. I am so sorry. I just don't seem to be able to get past Christmas without getting angry at Heavenly Father for taking Davy. I know all of the answers; it's just hard for me to feel the Christmas spirit in our circumstances. But I promise, starting tomorrow, I'll do better."

She kissed him back. He didn't notice the tears in her eyes, and he didn't hear her silent prayer. "It's a start. Thank you Heavenly Father. I will keep my end of this deal. I'll do better tomorrow, too."

Terri got into bed. This night she snuggled up to Jake. He put his arm around her, and they both quickly drifted off to their dreams.

❄ ❄ ❄

"Mommy, Daddy, let's go get the tree." Davy looked so cute and full of life. Terri ran to him and scooped him up into her arms. His hair was soft, and he hugged her as tightly as she hugged him. "You act like you haven't seen me in so long," he said. She could smell the fabric softener in his overalls.

"Let's put your shoes on, son. It's cold out there, and you know how picky your daddy is when it comes to his Christmas tree. We're going to be there awhile."

Davy giggled. He was so excited. Jake called from

outside, “Let’s get going you stragglers. All of the good trees will be gone by the time you’re ready to leave.”

“We’re coming, Daddy. Come on, Mom, let’s go.”

“All right, son, let’s go.”

The Christmas tree lot was prettier than ever. The trees were perfect. The cold wind blew through Davy’s blond hair.

“It’s going to be a tough choice this year.” Jake was talking to himself, but Davy and Terri both heard him.

“Let me pick the tree Daddy, please?”

“Oh please, Jake, I know you choose the tree, but let’s have Davy choose this year.”

“Well, okay. This time we’ll let Davy choose. Which one will it be?”

Davy walked around and around the lot until he finally stopped in front of “the” tree. “I want this one.”

“That one will be perfect. It’s just the right height.” Jake touched the top of Davy’s head. “You’re growing like a weed. You’ll be taller than me in no time, son.”

Everything was so perfect. “Now who is this?”

The girl standing close to Davy was precious. She had brown hair like Terri’s and big brown eyes. She looked like she was only two or three.

“Mom, you’re so silly.” Davy held the little girl’s hand like she was his dearest friend.

Jake called, “Terri, wake up. It’s morning.” The little girl vanished.

❄ ❄ ❄

"We must have been pretty tired. It's nearly 10:00 o'clock. I'll get breakfast ready and then I want to talk to you about something."

Terri was surprised to find herself in bed. "Just another dream," she thought. "It was so real." She got up and rolled to her knees to say her morning prayers. When she finished she put on her robe and went to the kitchen.

"Surprise!" Jake had already fixed breakfast, and he pulled out her chair so she could sit down.

"My" she said, "what's the occasion?" You haven't fixed a breakfast like this since . . . . "

"I know, since Davy died." Jake took her hands in his. She looked at his hands.

"I love your hands, Jake. I love you. Jake, I am so sorry for wasting all this time . . . . " Jake put his finger gently over her lips.

"I'm the one who's sorry. It's time to get on with our lives. Davy would want it that way. He loved us so much. He loved us as much as we love him. I believe he still does." Jake had tears in his eyes, but his face was happier than she had seen it in a long time. "Terri, what do you say we go buy a tree? I know it won't be the same, but I think we need a tree this year."

"That would be wonderful. I was thinking that myself."

"Well, hurry up and get dressed, you straggler; all the good ones will be gone." They both hurried as they ate their breakfast, and they smiled as they ate.

Their favorite tree lot was just where they had left it two Christmases ago. The same old trailer behind the same old building on Naples Hill. It was morning, but the lights strung from pole to pole burned brightly waiting for dark to enhance their beauty. Everything was the same as it had been the last time they bought their tree except the person who greeted them.

"Good morning," the young woman said. She was pretty, dressed in a large blue-patterned flannel shirt and worn Levi's, old but clean. "We really have some beautiful trees. Actually they're the prettiest I've ever seen. I'd like to buy one myself, they're so pretty."

"Well, that's why we come here every year to buy ours. Where's Old Dan? He usually takes care of us."

Old Dan was the owner, and he had made such a fuss over Davy. After they bought their tree, Old Dan gave Davy some hot chocolate and told him a story about Christmas. Davy seemed to love the story as much as shopping for a tree.

"He's right over there helping another customer. If you would rather, he can help you. He'll just be another minute; he's in the middle of one of his stories."

She started to walk away when the same blond-haired boy they had seen at the top of Naples Hill ran over to her to show her something he had in his hands.

"Mom, can I keep him? The lady in the front says I can have him if it's all right with you." He held a small, charcoal-colored puppy. "He's little now, but she says he'll get big real fast."

"Oh, Manny, what will we do with a puppy? There's hardly room for the two of us, let alone a . . . cute little, lonely little . . . Oh, Manny, what am I going to do with you?"

"Oh thank you, Mommy. I'll take care of him, and he can eat some of my food." The little boy squealed with joy. “This will be the best Christmas yet!”

Jake and Terri watched as the woman and her little boy found so much joy in such a small thing. In the bright morning air, they both gasped simultaneously as they saw the cold wind stream through the boy’s blond hair.

“I have an idea.” Jake turned to the boy.

“Manny, can you come over here and help me for a minute?” Manny looked at his mother, not sure what to do. Jake looked to the little boy’s mother for approval. She nodded to Manny, and he walked over to where Terri and Jake stood.

“We have a big problem, Manny. We need a great Christmas tree this year, and we just can’t seem to make up our mind which one to chose. Do you think you could help us pick it out?”

“Well, my mommy says I’m real good at picking out trees. Come over here.” There stood a giant Noble Fir. Its branches were perfectly formed except for one spot on the bottom. “You want this one?”

“I think he’s right. What do you think, Terri?”

“I agree.” She looked at Jake for a moment and their eyes met. Then she turned to the little boy and his mother.

“You really have helped us with this Christmas more than you could ever know. Would you consider coming to our house and spending Christmas Day with us? I know you don’t know us, but we would really like to have you in our home to help us celebrate.”

Old Dan piped up, “Sandy, they’re all right. I’ve been selling them trees for years. Well, come to think of it, I haven’t seen you in a couple of Christmases. And where is little . . . Davy-boy isn't it? Yeah, that's his name: Davy-boy. I've missed telling him stories about Christmas."

Terri shifted on her feet nervously, "He died two years ago, Dan. We've been having a pretty rough time of it since. This is our first tree since he died."

She took Jake's hand. "We've decided we have to go on. Davy would want us to."

"Well, Miss Sandy, I say these are good people. Go have Christmas with them. Besides, you don't really have a lot of alternatives."

Sandy shot Old Dan a look but he went on. "Miss Sandy and her boy are in kind of a bind. Mrs. Huntington has sold the building and will be taking the trailer with her when she moves to Oregon. They really don't have anywhere to go."

Sandy spoke up, "It would be wonderful if we didn't have to be back out in the cold air. Manny and I have been praying that something would happen to help us out. Thank you for your invitation, that is if you really mean it, and do you think you could handle a puppy for a day?"

It was Jake's turn to speak. "For a day nothing. You can stay as long as is necessary. We know some people who can help you find a good job, and then you'll be able to get a real place to stay. Please come to our house; it would mean a great deal to us. In fact why don't you both move in a little early, like today?"

"Well then, that's settled. Now come on over here and let me tell you all a little story about Christmas." And Old Dan did just that.

❄ ❄ ❄

Christmas morning Terri and Jake were the first

ones up. They could hardly wait for their guests to wake up. Finally Jake turned on the stereo very loud. "Joy to the World" filled the home. In a few minutes Manny and his mom came down to the living room.

"Merry Christmas, you two stragglers" said Jake. "Let's get to opening some of these presents."

The tree was crowded with presents, most of them for Manny, but there were plenty for Sandy, too.

Jake said, "We've been saving these presents for a long time. We're tired of waiting for them to be opened."

Manny couldn't believe his eyes. "Look, Mommy, Darth Vader. And Mommy, a bike! Is this really for me?"

"It is especially for you, Manny. They're all for you."

In a little while, all the presents had been opened and breakfast had been served. Jake and Terri watched the blond-haired boy and his mom out back trying out the new bike.

"It looks pretty empty under there. But wait a minute, what's this?" Jake took a small package from behind his back.

"I found this in Davy's dresser drawer last night," he said. "I had forgotten all about it. It's from Davy for you."

Terri took the present in her hands and pressed it to her heart. She closed her eyes for a moment and then slowly examined the present. There was a card. Carefully she opened it. It was written in Davy's nearly unreadable writing.

"I helped him with the spelling. He sure loved to write his letters. The words are all his."

The card read, "To the best mommy on Beech

Street. I love you. Thank you for taking good care of me. I hope you will have a Merry Christmas this year. Love, Davy-boy."

She opened the package. Tears fell from her eyes. Davy had drawn a picture. There was Jake with a big smile. There was Terri with an apron on, and she was holding a small bundle with brown hair like Terri's. And there was blond Davy smiling broadly.

Looking more closely at the drawing, Jake asked, "What is that you're holding?"

"I'm not sure. There's no way Davy could have known then about my present to you."

"What present? I don't see anything left under the tree. What are you talking about? I thought we had an agreement; our Christmas to each other would be sharing with Manny and Sandy." Jake was a little upset because he obviously had kept his side of the agreement.

"Jake, we're going to have a baby. And if I could guess, I would have to say it will be a little brown-eyed, brown-haired beauty. Merry Christmas, my dear."

Terri didn't miss on her guess.

— David S. Gibson

The Stars of Bethlehem

Grandmother Gibson's home was always warm, a fire crackling in the cast-iron stove. Her Christmas tree was always flocked white, except after Grandpa died; there was always an abundance of gifts, and nothing could change that. It was not any of these things that made Christmas morning special at Grandmother's, though. What made it special was that we were all there — everyone — Dad and Mom, brothers and sisters, aunts and uncles, cousins. Being all together, we enjoyed the warmth of Grandmother's smile. She gave so much joy at the hands of the home shopping channel, and even though some of the gifts had no practical use, they had come from her, with love. It was a love that feels like no other, except one.

Grandma Mary's home was always warm, the pilot always lit in the gas furnace; her tree was seldom white, nor ever as tall; there were not a lot of gifts under the tree, but there was at least one for each of us. We were all there — everyone — Mom and Dad, brothers and sisters, aunts and uncles, cousins. Grandma's smile was of the same warmth and tenderness earlier felt at Grandmother's house. Of her modest gifts, some had a practical use, and all were given with love. It was a love that felt like no other, except one.

These two wonderful women, the queens of the season, were my light and joy at Christmas time, as the sun is to the planets, orbiting in their spheres. They were the anchors of two wind-buffeted, battle-worn, and wave-tossed families. Near these anchors was the still water, and at Christmas time, it was not only still; it was clear.

Grandmother Gibson and Grandma Mary were much of what Christmas meant to me as a boy, but now they were gone. Within a month of each other during the holiday season, my two stars of Bethlehem were taken from me, and I found myself unable to find my way. Without their warmth, it looked to be for me, a cold, dark Christmas, if any Christmas at all.

I was not able to attend their funerals. I was in Southern Africa at the time; duty stood in the way of my paying tribute one last time to these virtuous women. They were both very proud of me and the work I was doing, and neither one would have had me leave it. That did not, however, give me much relief. I wanted to be there for them as they had always been there for me, and I couldn't.

My parents had married relatively young while my dad was still in college. As a result, Mom had to go to work. Finances were spread very thin; they were forced to live apart at times. Mom put in long, hard hours to help my dad through school. The devotion she showed, she had learned from many years of watching Grandma. Mom and Grandma were cut from the same pattern. I spent a lot of time being cared for by Grandma, and the bond I had with my mother was also shared with her.

As I grew and Dad got out of school, Grandma continued to be important to me. Her home was my home. She taught me to write. My penmanship continues to benefit me to this day when neatness is called for. She taught me to play simple songs on her piano that I can still play today. Though she was hard of hearing and sang slightly off key, she taught me songs that built my childhood faith. I owed it to her to be there to say goodbye, but I could not be there. Grandma was a forgiving debtor.

When I was young, I was not very healthy. The doctors could do little for me other than to stem the flow as the tide of my young life ran out. Grandmother had something else in mind. She was the family apothecary and knew in her faithful heart that, in a world as big and diverse as this, there must be some cure for a dying little boy. The doctors had painted a picture of a short life that would probably end before maturity. They stated flatly that even if I survived to adulthood, I would never father any children. So, Grandmother took another route. We went frequently to an herbalist she trusted, and as a result I look forward to a long and healthy life with as many children as I desire.

As Grandma had taught me to write legibly, Grandmother taught me proper diction. She constantly corrected my use of her beloved English language, and I thank her for it. Where Grandma had been able to teach me the words of songs, Grandmother taught me the notes they were set to; she had a beautiful voice. Grandmother was the other side of a two-headed coin that was invested in me at birth and built a fortune there. I owed it to her to be there to say goodbye, but I could not be there. Grandmother was a forgiving debtor.

So there I sat in Africa at Christmas time. December is summertime there. I had been invited to Christmas dinner with some friends, but instead of hot turkey and ham and all the fixings, there were a number of cold salads. Cold salad in Africa is anything one can find in the fridge mixed with an ample helping of mayonnaise. After dinner, everyone else headed off for the beach, and I went home to my one-room, lonely apartment. On my nightstand was the miserable excuse for a Christmas tree that was sold on the streets of Capetown. It consisted of a sickly bough cut from the strange breed of pine tree that grows in the cape area. It had no colored lights, no tinsel, no red and green orbs on it, and no gifts beneath it. It was a Christmas tree without the Christmas or the tree.

Pondering, I asked many questions. Why were they gone? Did they know how much love I had for them? Would I ever be able to embrace them again? Then I remembered what these two wonderful mothers had taught me throughout my life: Christmas was the celebration of the Son of God; with His birth came happiness; Christmas is a time for happiness. So why did I feel so sad?

I thumbed through the little collection of photographs I had. As I took in the images of family and friends, I stopped twice — at a picture of Grandma and one of Grandmother. The photos were taken when they both were a little younger, before disease had ravaged their bodies and taken the lives they clung determinedly to. There on their faces was the common smile they shared. Though made of paper, the photos touched me warmly, and the sensations I felt gave life to them in my mind's eye. My eyes found their way past the pictures to my miserable little tree. It had no star. Well, now it would have two. I grabbed two paper-clips and fastened my two stars to their places, and then, like the wise men, I could find my way.

The room began to glow in the radiance of that shared smile. Warmth flooded the room in a supernatural way as these two patron saints of Christmas, newly canonized, opened my mind to their vision of the Savior of mankind. They had been saviors to a small, sickly, blond-haired boy in his adolescence and were now becoming saviors of my love for Christmas. Tears filled my eyes in that rapturous moment, and falling to my knees, I thanked my God for sending two such guardians to me. I will forever bask in the warmth of their love each Christmas hence.

Now, as I see my son, I am grateful he will experience the same joy that I have. Cut from the same pattern as their mothers were, his guardians, be they called Grandma or Grandmother, will be his Christmas stars and our families' anchors. They are the Christmas spirit — a spirit of peace, of example, of kindness, of virtue, of unconditional love.

— David S. Gibson, Jr.

Do Unto Others . . .

Driving down the empty, late-night city streets, Jeremy Sanders had a lot on his mind. The winter night in the city was as bleak and lifeless as his thoughts. As he watched the furrows of dirty, salty slush pass by on either side of the road, the memory of a conversation he had with his former boss came fresh into his mind . . . .

It had been a warm summer day and had started like every other warm summer day. Jeremy had awakened just before his alarm chimed the six o'clock hour. He had showered and shaved, dressed in one of many fine suits hanging in his closet, kissed his wife, and eaten an apple on his way out the door. The drive to work was uneventful, and the normal morning traffic had not made him late. Sally, his secretary, had smiled when she saw him and had given him an itinerary for the day. Everything on the schedule had been normal except for a lunch that had been scheduled with Jack, his boss, at a downtown restaurant he had taken clients to for business luncheons.

Jeremy was steadily working his way up the corporate ladder. Accounting had been his chosen field, but being an excellent writer and public relations talent, he had changed his career path and now managed a few large corporate accounts. All of this had happened in his first three years out of school, and he was not yet long enough with the company to earn a commission. He was a salaried associate and was used to unpaid overtime. Hints had been dropped recently, however, to the effect that he may soon move up another rung into the lower end of the big money where hard work began to pay off — pay off things like school loans, a mortgage, two cars, and all the expense that comes with a two-year-old son who had been born prematurely. Jeremy was grateful that after sufficient medical attention, his son had recovered. Jack had been Jeremy's mentor and his information highway to the top. Was today the day?

❄ ❄ ❄

"Well, Jeremy, how is everything?" Jack, a casualty of the big-business, early-afternoon martini, was nursing his third drink.

"Trina is doing well and handling Josh okay." It was the normal small talk, except for Jack's three drinks, that started off all of their lunchtime meetings. "Things are actually going very well. The Jefferson account is coming along."

"Funny you should mention it. The Jefferson account is what this lunch is all about."

"Oh?" Miles Jefferson was a pompous idiot. He lived in another city, but flew in regularly, as Jack handled his accounts. Inherited wealth and inherited management of that wealth had transformed the reckless spender, young Miles Jefferson, into thrifty tightwad Miles T. Jefferson. Jeremy had been intimidated slightly when Jack assigned him the account, but he bit the bullet and formed what he thought to be a professional working relationship . . . until the previous Friday night.

The phone had rung at 11:30 that night. Exhausted from a long week, Jeremy had gone to bed as soon as he had arrived home — an hour earlier. It was Jefferson on the other end of the line, his voice slurred as the result of a drinking binge that had begun earlier in the day. He said he was in town and wanted some excitement. He had called Jeremy and asked him to line him up with a "woman of the night," as he had called it. Jeremy, appalled, had told Jefferson to sober up and hung up the phone. At lunch the next day, Jefferson had apologized, and Jeremy thought the incident would be forgotten.

"Why didn't you just get him a girl, Jer?" Jack asked, seriously.

"We aren't an escort service, Jack. You know I don't use those tactics. I don't drink, I don't cheat, and I don't help others to either. Besides, Jefferson apologized and dropped the whole thing last week," Jeremy answered defensively.

"Well, buddy-boy, he picked it back up this week, and you, my friend, are out of a job. Pick up your check tonight when you leave."

"Is this some kind of joke, Jack? Please tell me you're kidding me."

Jack's eyes remained cold, if a little bloodshot. "No, Jeremy, it's no joke. You should have gotten him a girl."

"Mail me the check, Jack. I'm out of here right now," Jeremy said, standing — furious. "If you want me, I'll be down the street, working for your competition." Jeremy turned toward the exit.

"Wait a minute, Jeremy. There's something else you should know." Jack blurted.

"What's that?"

"Jefferson already took his account over there. He has been souring the well, kind of quiet-like, for you all over, all week long. There isn't a major firm he hasn't invested in — except ours now — and you have been blacklisted, buck-o."

"What?!" The blood was racing in Jeremy's veins right up to his head, and the anger was obvious on his face. "He can't do that!"

"He already did, Jeremy. You are a little fish, and he is a shark. Money talks, man." Jack finished his martini and signaled for another.

Jeremy got his wallet out and dropped his share of the check on the table. "I think it stinks, Jack." Jeremy left Jack there where he sat and headed for his office.

Thirty minutes later, he was on the road headed for home. Along the way, he had exhausted the numbers in his diary, and the response had been the same at the other end of every call: "Sorry, Jeremy. I haven't got anything for you." By the time he pulled into his driveway, a cloud had settled over him. Trina knew something was wrong when she heard his car door shut. She met him as he entered the house.

"Jeremy, what's wrong?" She crossed to him, and he slumped into her arms.

"I was fired this afternoon. Jack took me to lunch, got drunk, and gave me my walking-papers."

"Honey, why? You kill yourself for them every day."

"Jefferson. Do you remember what I told you last week?" She was nodding in reply. "Well, he didn't drop it. He has single-handedly ruined me in the last week.

What are we going to do?"

"We don't need them, Jeremy. You're talented and educated. Surely someone could use a good accountant."

"I called everyone I could think of, Trina, and they all turned me down."

"Then you can start your own firm."

Jeremy cut her off. "With what? You need capital, honey. We're already in debt up to our ears. Besides the little we've saved, we have nothing but liabilities. No bank is going to finance me, especially when Jefferson has got money in all of them."

They both stood there, hopeless, in each others arms for a long time.

❄ ❄ ❄

At a stoplight, Jeremy let his engine idle. The heater didn't work very well, and his spine tingled with a shiver. Trina's car had been nearly paid for, but Jeremy's sportier car still had a year's worth of payments left on it. They had sold Trina's car for the low blue-book price and were able to pay off Jeremy's. Using it as a trade in, and with some of what they had left from the sale of Trina's car, they bought a used car. That had given enough relief for groceries and the mortgage the first month. Unable to afford a babysitter, and considering Josh's fragile health, Trina had not been able to go to work.

Jeremy had met Trina in college. They had a lot in common: they were both only children, they were both putting themselves through school, and they had both recently lost their parents. The latter had become the foundation of an emotional bond that quickly grew into a romantic love. Trina's parents had been killed in a car wreck on the icy roads of their Colorado hometown. Jeremy's father had been killed by friendly fire as a tank commander in the Gulf War, and his mother, having a congenital heart defect, had died of natural causes. They literally had no family to turn to.

Jeremy had been able to collect unemployment for a few months, but it too had run out when he was hired by a temporary employment agency in town. Minimum wage and the last unemployment check had barely paid the bills, supplemented by their meager savings. Now, their account was nearly empty, and Jeremy was faced with something he had never seen in his plans for the future: Bankruptcy was knocking at his door.

The streetlight changed and interrupted his thoughts.

Rounding the corner, Jeremy started down the boulevard that led to the freeway, and an hour later, home. As he increased his speed, something off to the right caught his eye. He slowed slightly and his eyes came to rest on a gnarled, bent old man in rags, making his way up the icy walk toward an alley. A strange thing happened then: An overwhelming urge to help this man asserted itself in Jeremy's mind.

Shaking his head to clear his mind, Jeremy said to himself, "I'm practically homeless myself . . . . " But the thought was pushed aside as soon as it had been expressed. No, he knew he needed to help this man. He stopped his car and got out. Approaching the man, Jeremy realized that he was not as old as he had appeared. Closer to forty than sixty, this man was the picture of hopelessness. “Excuse me. Do you need some help?” Jeremy asked.

The man stopped and turned toward Jeremy. “Yes, please.” The man’s voice was humble and mild. “I need to get to the 10th Street shelter. Have you got some change to spare for the bus?”

Jeremy could smell alcohol on the man’s breath and started to second-guess his first instinct. Before he could say anything, the overwhelming feeling to help the man reasserted itself and Jeremy offered, “I have no money, and I’m not headed that way. The buses only stop on the hour here anyway, and it’s ten after right now. How about you come home with me?”

Jeremy could not believe his own ears. Had he just offered to take a homeless man, a complete stranger, into his home? What would Trina say? "What is your name, sir?"

"My name is Bill Jones. But I couldn't possibly accept your offer. We are complete strangers and . . . . "

"My name is Jeremy Sanders," Jeremy cut in, "and now were not complete strangers. We have been introduced."

"Well, Okay, but just for the night. Will you be back in the city tomorrow?"

"Yes, I can take you wherever you wish tomorrow. However, I must insist that you accept my hospitality tonight."

"Thank you, Mr. Sanders."

"It's Jeremy."

"Thank you, Jeremy." The gratitude could clearly be heard in his voice.

❄ ❄ ❄

Trina had not liked the idea at first, but Jeremy explained to her the feeling he had, and she seemed to understand. Their cupboards were nearly bare, but Trina was an excellent hostess, and like the mother she was, she had managed to put something warm and filling together for dinner. Jeremy had given Bill some of his clothes, and Bill had showered for the first time in a long time.

Dinner conversation was not much, but Bill had come to some understanding of the Sanders' situation from bits and pieces of quiet conversation between Jeremy and Trina heard through the wall of the adjacent room they had made up for him. Amazed at their generosity despite their situation, Bill drifted off with a feeling of love for his hosts.

After a small breakfast, Jeremy drove Bill to the shelter as asked.

"Bill?" Jeremy asked. "Are you sure this is all right? Isn't there something else that I can do for you?"

Bill pondered the question for a minute and answered, "No, Jeremy. You've already done much more than most would. I'll be fine."

"Do you have any family, Bill?"

"Yes. A brother. He lives in another city. He has a good job and a family. I haven't seen or spoken to him in years, though."

"Surely he would help you if he knew where you were. Can't we contact him?"

"I don't have a phone number or the money to call. I do have an address, though. I've been trying to save up for a bus ticket, but I drank away most of the money I earned."

"How much is that?"

"Oh, about eighty dollars." Bill started for the shelter door.

"Wait a minute, Bill." Again, Jeremy could not believe what he was about to say, but the feeling was back, and despite having only one hundred dollars to his name, he found himself offering it. "Let's go get that ticket for you."

Bill just stood there, dumbfounded at the generosity of this man he had met only the previous evening. He knew that Jeremy and his wife were completely broke.

They would be coming to the shelter themselves next week for all he knew. But, sensing Jeremy's resolution, he accepted.

❄ ❄ ❄

Jeremy had thought that Trina would kill him; she was amazingly calm, though. She knew inside that her husband had done the right thing.

A few weeks passed, and Christmas Eve came. The Sanders were spending what they thought to be their last days in their home. Holding each other close, Jeremy and Trina tried not to dwell on the rotten run of luck that had ruined every material aspect of their lives. Around ten o'clock, there was a knock at the door.

"I wonder who that could be," Jeremy said, getting up and answering the door. After a moment, Jeremy recognized the man on his doorstep as Bill. He seemed taller, was definitely cleaner, was wearing a business suit, and was not alone. Behind him stood a man who Jeremy never thought he would see again. It was Jefferson.

"Jeremy," Bill said, "I would like you to meet my brother, Miles."

"We've met. In fact, I used to work for him." Jeremy did not know what else to say.

"May we come in?" Miles asked. "I know how this must look to you, but I want to tell you something."

"Yes, come in. Trina, this is Miles T. Jefferson."

Trina stood, staring unbelievably.

"Jeremy," Miles began, "I'm sorry for the grief your family has suffered these last months. But, I had to be sure that you were what you seemed to be."

"What?" Jeremy asked. "I don't think I understand your meaning."

"Let me explain, Jeremy. I was impressed with your integrity from the beginning. I need someone like you to manage my affairs. I am worth hundreds of millions of dollars, and I need to be able to trust the chief executor of all my assets."

"What are you saying, Mr. Jefferson?" Jeremy's head was spinning.

"I am saying that I want you to take care of my finances. I want you to hire other trustworthy people to work for me. I want to make sure that you are set for life because I know that you're the kind of person who gives and gives, serves and serves, and that's the kind of person I want working for me. What do you say?"

❄ ❄ ❄

That night, Jeremy and Trina spent a long time on their knees thanking God for their blessings, asking Him to always help them to follow their hearts, and giving thanks for a happy ending to their Christmas Eve.

— David S. Gibson, Jr.

Samuel's Wall

"How did I ever get into this mess?" She knew the answer and regretted asking the question. She had seen the young Lamanite Prophet jump from the great wall of the city. Ever since then she had called the place Samuel's Wall.

She had run to help him find his balance when he had stumbled, and he had thanked her as he ran away to escape. Of course she had only been eleven years old at that time, but even then she knew he spoke the truth.

Five years had passed since that memorable week when Samuel had made that glorious prophecy about the birth of Jesus, the Savior. But now she was a prisoner and would be put to death if the foretold event she waited for did not occur.

She looked around the cell. Each of the people held in the small dark room were people she had known most of her life. As far as she knew, they would all stand firm to the end. Three of the men had taught her parents about Jesus. One of the women had seen her help the young Lamanite to his feet when he had jumped from the wall.

Each person in the small group had believed in the prophecy of the Savior's birth and, in fact, shared those beliefs with others. Now it all came down to this. The signs of His birth must appear tomorrow. They must! Or all of them would be put to death.

When she was first detained, she had been offered

her freedom because she was young and because she was a girl. She had looked questioningly into the eyes of the soldier.

"You will let me go because I am young? Cannot the young believe?" She had asked. She then answered her own question, "Of course we can. Being young, being a girl is no barrier to a knowledge of the truth. I believe the Savior will be born as was prophesied. I cannot deny it."

She could still hear the frustrated words of the soldier, "You young fool! I will let you go if you will be silent. You don't have to deny it out loud, just be silent and go free."

She spoke from the heart, without a thought as to the consequences, "I am a free Nephite with the right to speak. What good is that right if I cannot speak the truth? I shall not be silent, for I believe He will surely come."

There. She had said it. She realized, now too late, that she was a bit outspoken. Her mother had been right.

The soldier answered, "Very well, we will see how loud you beg for your life tomorrow when you are exposed for the fool you are. You can die with the rest of the fools. You could have gone free, but no more. The only way you will go free now is if you admit your lies publicly with the rest of your friends."

The others were surprised to see her cast in with them. They thought she had hidden with her family. Young people were not customarily punished this way even in this wicked day and age. And a girl! Surely they would not punish a girl. But nevertheless, there she was waiting with the rest.

As she looked at each of the people in the room, she noticed they all were more than a little scared. "Do you think they will really kill us as they claim they will do?" She asked the others.

"We will fight them," said Joshua, one of the larger men in the room.

"Why not just do as they ask?" suggested Nathan. "What is there to gain from dying? We cannot control when or if the Messiah comes with our simple statements."

She again spoke before she had time to think, "I believe He will come as the Prophets have declared, and I will not deny it. It does make a difference to me!"

From the corner of the room, Benjamin cried out, "What do you know about making a difference? You are just a girl, barely old enough to have any responsibility. These people have families that must live on. How will they do that if we die for nothing?" The man shook with anger, and his eyes bore into her like a pointed stick.

Slowly, she replied, "Benjamin, I am sorry that my words offended you. Courage is important to me. But more than anyone here, you know of courage. Our families are hiding, but your family is dead. I saw your wife Tama look the soldiers in the eye and testify of Christ who is to come. She knew her words would mean her own death as well as your son's. I watched and listened as you begged the soldiers to spare her, even offering to trade places with her and your son." Tears spilled down her face, and emotion choked off her words to the angry man.

All she could do was put her arms around him and hug him. It helped her as much as it did him. When he looked up again, his face was softer; his mood was calm. "Thank you. You made me think." All of the people in the small dark room thought.

Half an hour before the sun was to set, the soldiers came for their prisoners. The little band was marched to the top of the city wall to the very place where the young Lamanite had stood five years earlier. All of the leaders of the unbelievers were present, watching triumphantly at the spectacle about to take place.

Out of the corner of her eye, the young girl saw the troubled face of the soldier who had spoken so roughly to her the day before. "Bring the girl first!" shouted the captain of the guard. Two soldiers grabbed her arms and started forward with her.

"Wait, I will take her." The soldier from yesterday came forward and took the girl from the others. As he walked her forward he whispered, "Please, renounce. They will kill you. Do you really believe Jesus can save you?"

Her answer was calm and sure. "Oh yes, He can save me, and He will. Maybe not here, maybe not today, but He will save me without any doubt. Do you really think that killing us can stop the birth of the Son of God, or the faith of those who wait for His coming? Yes, He will save me, and if you ask Him to forgive you for what you are about to do, He will save you, too."

"I wish I could believe again," he answered. "I heard the Lamanite too. And I did believe for a long time. It is just that it has taken so long, my faith has weakened."

"Stop talking there, and bring her here to the spot. It is just about time," shouted the captain. "Let us show the inhabitants of this city how we deal with these liars. Young girl, renounce your belief in this Jesus and I will let you return to your family wherever they are hidden."

Laughter from the crowd below drowned out the captain's words. He held up his arms to silence the unruly mob. "Now then give us your answer, and make sure it is the right one, for the sun is almost down and it is time to settle all of this."

The young girl looked out over the crowded plaza below the great wall. Angry faces stared at her waiting to hear her embarrassment as she backed down from the testimony that put her here on top of Samuel's Wall. She thought of her mother and father. She would not see them again in this life. But they would know that their daughter did not deny her testimony of Jesus.

Then, in her mind a vision suddenly formed. She could see a manger in a faraway place. There were animals and children and shepherds. In the middle of all of this, she could see a mother holding a child. She could see a father standing by, keeping watch over his little family. She heard beautiful music and she saw glorious angels.

"Fear not," she said to the others, "It has happened. He is born." She knelt before her executioner without fear, for she knew that it was all true. She was not afraid to die, for her death would be meaningful.

"Kill her!" Went up the cry.

"Hold!" shouted the soldier who had walked her to the spot on Samuel's Wall. "The sun goes down but the sky gets brighter. It is all true! Don't touch this brave girl. Let her go. Let her friends go too!"

It was true. The sun had set behind the mountains,

yet the darkness did not come. Instead of darkness, the sky stayed bright as noon day. The brightness did not pass away all that night nor through the next day. Surely this was the sign the Lamanite had prophesied five years before from this very spot, this place the young girl called Samuel's Wall. Everywhere people fell to their knees, crying in fear. But the young girl was not afraid. She cried tears of thanks.

Among the Nephites there were many tales told of brave men who protected the great city from its enemies. But always there would be told the story of the brave young girl who was protected by her God on Samuel's Wall.

— David S. Gibson

The End

Toby Whitaker closed the den door as quietly as he could. His wife and children were in bed, and these few moments were what he had been looking forward to all day. Sure, Toby enjoyed his family, and the bustle of Christmas shopping, baking, and decorating the house were great; but these evenings, tucked away in his den, were extra special. In the quiet of a late evening, Toby loved to seek out a bit of solitude and immerse himself in what he thought of as the very essence of Christmas. It was on such nights that Toby carried out his annual tradition of reading Charles Dickens' "A Christmas Carol."

Now, it was only ten days until Christmas, and the Dickens' tale had been completed more than a week ago. Tonight, Toby retired to the den with a new bit of yuletide reading before him. As he looked around the room, he nodded his head in satisfaction, a slight smile on his lips. The room lights were dimmed, and on the walls danced the glow of several red and green candles. Settling into the big overstuffed chair that Toby had proclaimed the most comfortable piece of furniture ever built, he made sure that his cup of hot chocolate topped with a mountain of whipped cream and the plate of far too many Danish butter cookies were both well within easy reach.

These details attended to, he carefully studied the book sitting in his lap. It was a large book, the size of a family Bible. The cover was of a rich, cordovan-hued leather, ornately carved and tooled. He let his fingers travel across the ridges and valleys of the intricate workmanship. Gold lettering in an Olde English font announced the book's title: "A Christmas Especially for You."

Toby wondered for whom the book had originally been written. Searching, he could not find any reference to the author's name in the volume. No name was printed on the cover, on the end spine, or on the title page beneath the cover. Maybe he'd ask his Uncle Wayne about it the next time he saw him, for it was his uncle who had given him the book.

With his mother's brother in mind, Toby's thoughts drifted back to the night before, when he had received the book. Uncle Wayne had invited him over for dinner. Toby dearly loved his uncle. The old gentleman was the most warmhearted and charitable person he had ever known. They had had a nice long conversation after the meal, chatting about many things, including Toby's mother. He had told his uncle how she was doing, what the doctors said about her health, and what the latest news was from the convalescent home where she lived. He remembered his uncle looking down at the floor and frowning a bit. Toby's stomach had tensed a little, fearing that a judgmental comment was forthcoming. But no such words were spoken. Uncle Wayne never did make such statements. Instead, his uncle had pushed himself up out of his chair and told Toby that he had something for him. He was gone from the room for several minutes, and when he returned he was carrying a scarf-wrapped bundle. Removing the cloth, he lovingly ran his fingers over the Christmas book's cover, and then held it out to his nephew.

"Here. This is for you," Uncle Wayne had stated quietly.

Given his uncle's tone and the loving way he handled the book, Toby knew that he was being given something quite precious.

Toby quoted the book's title, " 'A Christmas Especially for You.' It's beautiful. Thank you so much. Are you sure you want to do this?"

With a firm conviction in his voice that somewhat surprised Toby, his uncle answered, "Oh yes. I'm quite sure I want to do this." Looking his nephew in the eyes, he added, "If you'll read these stories through," and pointing a finger at his nephew to emphasize the next words, he continued, "*to the very end*, your Christmases will never be the same again."

There was almost a prophetic tone to his uncle's words, and Toby quickly responded, "Oh, I'll start reading tonight. I love Christmas stories."

For awhile his uncle said nothing, simply staring into the fire that flickered upon the hearth. In the midst of his pondering, he slowly shifted his gaze to his nephew and counseled, "This book is rather unique. These stories may not be as easily finished as you think." The older man paused, and then added, "But I'll promise you this: there is a happy ending to each and every tale — and if you'll persist, you can read them all. Nothing short of that will do."

Uncle Wayne turned again to study the glowing embers. This was getting quite mysterious. Toby just looked at him, waiting for him to continue, but apparently he'd said all he intended to say. Toby thanked him again for the present, and got up to leave, feeling more than a little bewildered. As he rose, his uncle took him by the shoulders, and with a loving, kindhearted look that seemed to penetrate to the very depths of Toby's soul, said, "Do what you must to finish the book. It will be well worth the effort."

Toby just nodded blankly.

By the time he arrived home, it was after midnight. Any attempt at reading would only result in him falling asleep, so Toby decided to put off starting the book until the next night.

And now, here he was, ready to begin the book which, according to his uncle, would change Christmas forever. That was quite a promise. A promise that he had mixed feelings about, for there really wasn't anything wrong with his Christmases as they were. This book must really be something.

Toby discovered that the book was not a single novel, but rather a collection of Christmas stories. He was soon engrossed in the first tale, a story of yuletide sharing and giving, filled to overflowing with the spirit of the season. The story told of a family that had fallen upon hard times. For them, there was not much to be cheerful about this Christmas season: no money for presents or festive trimmings, barely enough for a few daily scraps of food and a bit of coal to warm themselves.

Toby took a sip of hot chocolate and continued reading:

For eight-year-old Christopher, the hardest thing was knowing that there would be no Christmas tree. That was his very favorite part of Christmas. Every day he would go to the Christmas tree lot near his home and slowly walk up and down the rows of trees. He would breathe in deeply, drinking in the wonderful pine scent. Over and over, he would pretend that he was in the middle of a huge Christmas tree forest.

The old man that ran the lot had noticed Christopher's frequent visits. He had taken stock of the boy's hole-ridden shirt and pants and the meager scarf where there should have been a warm coat. The elderly gentleman was also aware that the boy's family had never been to the lot, and that probably meant that there was no Christmas tree in their home. He visualized nothing but an empty corner where there should have been a brightly lit tree with colorfully wrapped gifts beneath it. But this year, for this family, there would be no such things, no such celebration.

The old man looked at his watch. Seven o'clock, straight up: time to close. He looked at the small boy who was staring up at a particularly tall tree.

"Hey kid, you need to go home now. I've gotta close up. Christmas Eve, you know."

The boy met the man's gaze. Turning back for one final look at the tree, Christopher lowered his head and slowly shuffled toward the exit. As the youngster went through the gate, he kept his head down, not looking up at the old man.

The Christmas tree vendor watched the boy trod heavily down the dimly lit street. Shaking his head, he snapped the gate's lock shut and went home to his own family for a wonderful Christmas celebration. Their parlor was adorned by the prettiest tree on the lot.

The End

"What?!" Toby exclaimed out loud. He reread the final paragraph three more times. That couldn't be the end of the story. He turned the page, only to find the beginning of the next story. He went back and turned through every page of the tale, examining each one carefully to make sure he hadn't missed anything. No way! This couldn't be right. This just wasn't the way the story should end. In fact, it was a perfectly stupid, ridiculous, and crazy ending.

Toby flipped the page, intent on starting the second story, anxious to see if it was written like a Christmas story should be written. He was interrupted by the phone ringing. At this late hour it could only be one person: his mother. She just didn't understand that not everyone got a brand new energy boost at eleven o'clock at night like she did. She wasn't a bit tired, so it didn't make sense that anyone else should be. From her perspective, now was the perfect time for a nice long chat with one of her children. After all, they didn't come to visit her all that much, so this was a good way of keeping in touch.

Toby was able to keep the call down to a mere twenty minutes. Telling his mother that he loved her, vowing to do a better job of keeping in touch, and promising that he would come visit sometime during the next week, he said goodbye and hung up the phone.

For several minutes he sat in the chair, lost in thoughts of his mother. Her situation presented a whole set of problems that he'd been trying desperately to avoid thinking about. Fourteen months ago, Agnes Whitaker had suffered a stroke. Toby's brother and his wife had taken her into their home and tried caring for her. That had only lasted for a couple of months. The intensity of care demanded by his mother's condition was just too much for them, and they had reluctantly decided to place her in a rest home. The doctors' prognosis was that there would be no significant recovery. They expected that she would continue to weaken and would undoubtedly need to remain in a full-care facility, like the Rosewood Convalescent Home, for the remainder of her life.

The wrinkle in this whole scenario came when Agnes Whitaker had started getting better. Just when she was supposed to be weakening, she began getting stronger. The partial speech loss she had suffered with the stroke was all but gone, her appetite was returning, and, lately, she spoke of returning to her home. But her health was still considered fragile, and that, coupled with her age, put living by herself out of the question. The option of living with family members would soon be reentering the picture. There would be no real reason for staying at the convalescent center.

Toby drew a deep breath and blew it out. He had entertained these thoughts before. And it was always at this point in his thinking that he decided not to think about it anymore . . . at least for the time being. There were too many obstacles, problems, and challenges to have to think about. And, besides, there really wasn't any urgency to the situation. The staff at Rosewood took good care of his mother, and she was getting better. Of course, that was the stickler; she was getting a lot better.

Toby shook his head. His thoughts had just brought him full circle, without coming any closer to feeling better about things. It was the same circle he'd been running in for over a month now. Unexpectedly, he pictured the look on Uncle Wayne's face when they'd spoken of his mother. That look had bothered him then, and it was still bothering him. What was it his uncle hadn't been willing to say aloud? Toby's thoughts drifted to the fact that it was right after that look that Uncle Wayne had produced the book. The book — ah yes! — the book. All thoughts of his mother were swept from Toby's mind as a renewed irritation grew over that ridiculous Christmas tree story. Time to get on with — the book.

As Toby read the opening paragraphs of the second story, his optimism and good spirits were rekindled. This was his favorite kind of Christmas story, something that could have come straight from the pen of Charles Dickens. It was set on a crisp December night in the bustling holiday-filled streets of Victorian-era London. Golden light emanated from the window panes of countless shops, each trimmed with holly, mistletoe, and ivy, and all of them crowded with shoppers and storekeepers in the merriest of dispositions.

The tale was a love story . . . .

Mr. Quigley was a funny little man. He took tiny, quick steps when he walked, his arms shuffled back and forth like the fly rods of a steam engine's wheel, and his glasses were forever finding their way right to the tip of his nose. He was quite proud to be the owner of the oldest bookstore in Camden town. Things were always tidy in Mr. Quigley's shop. Never a book out of place, never a speck of dust disgracing a shelf, never a title that he couldn't locate immediately. In fact, all of Mr. Tidus J. Quigley's life was quite this orderly. Confusion was simply not to be tolerated.

Today would prove to be an exception to this rule. It was on the afternoon of December 24th, Christmas Eve, when Jacob T. Dawson entered the store, hat in hand, and announced that he wished to speak with Mr. Quigley.

The visit was not unexpected. Mr. Quigley's daughter had forewarned him that the young man who had been courting her would be coming by the shop, and that he had something very important to discuss with Mr. Quigley. From the look in his daughter's eyes, and the frequent company the young couple had been keeping, he suspected that a marriage proposal was at hand. Young Jacob was undoubtedly coming by to seek his permission and blessing.

Quite enjoying the look of nervous misery etched upon Jacob's face, Mr. Quigley decided to say nothing, but simply stared at Jacob, playfully prolonging the boy's agony. Despite Jacob's best of intentions, things didn't go well at all. Emphasizing his great love and devotion to Emilia Quigley, Jacob swung his arms out and nearly knocked over a book display that Quigley had just finished putting together. Somehow, he got the words out and asked for Mr. Quigley's permission to marry his daughter.

Placing his hands on the young man's shoulders, and with a smile on his face, Mr. Quigley told Jacob that he would be honored to have him as a son-in-law. Jacob was so happy he didn't know what to do.

Just then the shop door opened and Emilia Quigley rushed in. Jacob's heart nearly stopped. The white fur of her hooded cape framed her face, giving her the most angelic appearance Jacob had ever seen. There was a smile on her face and excitement in her eyes. This was going to be the best Christmas that Jacob could possibly have imagined, betrothed to his beautiful Emilia.

The young girl hurried to her father and gave him a hug. "Oh Father. I'm so happy."

Squeezing his daughter tightly, he looked over at Jacob and smiled. "Me too, sweetheart."

Emilia looked up at her father in surprise. "How could you have possibly known? Arthur Bobbington only asked me to marry him but a few minutes ago. And I said yes. Oh, I'm so happy! I must go tell mother."

And without another word, Emilia ran out the front door, leaving the two men staring at each other. Perhaps this wouldn't be the best Christmas Jacob T. Dawson had ever had.

The End

"No way! Not again!" Toby slammed the book shut, bolting upright in his chair. Another story ending that made absolutely no sense. These weren't Christmas stories at all. They were a bad joke. They were complete nonsense; that's what they were. Toby paced back and forth, mumbling to himself.

"The guy has a Christmas tree lot full of trees and it's Christmas Eve. It's over, for Pete's sake. He's not going to sell any more. And he won't even give one to the poor little kid who's practically crying because his family doesn't have a tree. All the old geezer can say is 'Get out kid. I gotta go home to my Christmas party . . . By the way, you should see how big our tree is.' What a jerk!"

By nature Toby was somewhat excitable, and his nature was certainly showing through.

"And this Arthur Bobbington dude — where did he come from? That was by far the dumbest story I've ever read."

Looking down at the closed book, he sarcastically repeated the title, " 'A Christmas Especially for You.'

Right! Well, whoever wrote this thing must have had his worst enemy in mind." Shaking his head in disgust, he turned the den light off and went to bed.

The next day, Toby couldn't keep his mind off of the book. Its distorted tales were constantly trespassing on his thoughts. The company Christmas tree was right outside his door, an arrangement which, until now, he'd found quite enjoyable. But today, every time he saw the tree he thought of the small boy with his head hung low, walking away from the Christmas tree lot . . . sobbing. Toby frowned as he realized that the story hadn't said anything about the boy crying. It didn't matter. In Toby's imagination, the youngster was now wailing quite loudly.

In the hall, he passed a group of women wrapped in animated conversation over an upcoming marriage. They were discussing how the reception decorations would involve creating a winter wonderland. Toby purposely stopped and turned around to see what the bride-to-be looked like. Sourly he thought, "I wonder how many guys she jilted on her way to the altar . . . Poor Jacob T. Dawson."

Reality again took hold, and Toby realized how ridiculous these thoughts were. He promised himself that he wouldn't think about the book again for the rest of the day. It didn't work. By the time the work day was over, Toby could hardly wait to get to the third story. Maybe it would be better. It wasn't.

That night he read of a little girl who had been wishing for one special dolly all year long. The store sold the last one an hour before her mother got there. *"The End."* He read of a boy who had saved every penny he'd earned for the past six months in order to buy just the right gift for his mother. On the way to the shop, he tripped and his money was lost down a storm drain. *"The End."*

That second night as Toby closed the book, he didn't pace the room ranting and raving. He was just as unsettled by the disappointing endings, but his mood was more somber. That night, the hot chocolate and Danish butter cookies went untouched as he sat in his chair lost in thought.

The gleam in his Uncle's eye and the assurance in his face were totally inconsistent with what he'd found in the book. Uncle Wayne had seemed so excited to give him the book, and had such glowing praise for it. Why? So far, Toby hadn't found anything uplifting about the thing. All it had done was ruin two perfectly good evenings, not to mention a work day when his mood had seemed to grow more sour by the minute.

Toby decided to call his Uncle and talk to him about the mysterious book. When his uncle answered, he didn't seem the least bit surprised to be hearing from Toby. The nephew explained each story, raising his voice and talking rapidly each time he recounted one of the strange endings. His uncle listened patiently without interrupting. When Toby had finished, he paused, expecting some explanation from his uncle. He was surprised when the older man simply replied:

"That's very interesting. How's your mother?"

The question was so unexpected that, even though he'd heard his uncle quite clearly, Toby's only response was, "What?"

"How's your mother?" Toby noticed that the question was repeated with an exaggerated slowness this time.

"She's fine, I guess. I talked to her the night after we had dinner." Toby answered.

"Oh, you called her?" his uncle asked.

"No, she called me."

"Oh."

Toby thought he detected a disappointed tone in his uncle's voice, although he couldn't imagine why.

"Anyway, about this book . . . " Toby began again.

His uncle interrupted, "Toby, don't worry about it; you just haven't made it through to the ending yet. Work a little harder to catch the Christmas spirit, my boy. That'll do the trick. Talk to your mother. Maybe she'll have some ideas. Never have met anyone who loves Christmas quite as much as your mother, you know."

"But . . . " Toby began to protest.

"Well, it's been nice chatting with you. Call again soon. Give my love to your mother. Goodbye." And Uncle Wayne was gone.

That was about the most frustrating phone call he had ever had. Toby began suspecting his uncle's sanity, but that was ridiculous. Uncle Wayne was as sharp as a tack. His uncle hadn't seemed at all surprised or concerned about the out-of-place story endings. He'd talked as if it were no big problem at all: " . . . you just haven't made it through to the ending yet. Work a little harder to catch the Christmas spirit." What in the world did all that mean?

Maybe his uncle meant that he had to get to the very end of the book before things would make sense. He decided to try a shortcut. Skipping to the final story,

Toby began reading . . . great! A bunch of elves had gotten lost, and, unless they were rescued, they weren't going to make it back to the North Pole in time to help Santa load his sleigh, and Christmas would be ruined. A friendly polar bear was cast to be their rescuer, but in the final paragraph of the story . . . .

> *A terrible storm arose. With the wind howling and blinding snow swirling everywhere, the polar bear and all of the elves headed off in the wrong direction.*
>
> *The End*

"Oh, that was a lot of help," Toby muttered to himself, slapping the book shut.

He sat in his chair thinking until well past midnight. When Toby finally arose and shuffled off to bed, he found that he had been thinking more of his mother than of the book. He remembered the wonderful Christmases she had made for him and his brothers. He recalled how excited she became once Thanksgiving had passed, and it was time for Christmas to "officially begin," as she would say. As Toby glanced back at his candlelit den, hot chocolate, and Christmas cookies, he thought that his mother would probably enjoy sharing in his annual quest for the pure essence of Christmas.

He roused from his nostalgia. This last thought had brought him a little too close to the guilt that lingered about his mother's continued confinement at the Rosewood Convalescent Home. Time to go to bed.

During the night, Toby was abruptly awakened by the thought that perhaps the Christmas book was magical. Chalking it up as the rambling of a dream, Toby rolled over and went back to sleep. But the same thought greeted him again the next morning, the instant he woke up.

It was a crazy idea. Still, several of Uncle Wayne's comments fell right in line with the notion, like matching pieces of a jigsaw puzzle. The night Toby had received the book, his uncle had said that it was "rather unique," and that the stories "may not be as easily finished as you think." Letting his imagination run free, Toby wondered: What if the story endings he had been reading weren't the real endings? What if somehow they could change?

He shook his head and let out a short laugh at his own foolishness. Such thinking was silly, and he knew it. But, on the other hand, the thought was fascinating. And, he rationalized, since the whole idea was based on the premise that the book was enchanted, then what the heck. Magic could do whatever magic wanted to, couldn't it? Toby gave a short bob of his head signifying that he agreed with himself.

More of his uncle's comments came to mind. His promise that, "there's a happy ending to each and every tale — and if you'll persist, you can read them all." And Uncle Wayne's parting words that evening had been, "Do what you must to finish the book." Then last night, when his uncle had so lightly dismissed Toby's concern over the story endings, his off-the-cuff solution had been for the younger man to "work a little harder to catch the Christmas spirit."

Toby raised his eyebrows and sat up a little straighter as he began to focus on the pattern of his uncle's words: "persist . . . do what you must . . . work a little harder." All of these spoke directly of Toby taking some action. And all of the counsel had been directed at finishing the book, at reading the stories through to the end. Maybe, thought Toby, that is the way the story endings are changed — by him doing something or other. No sooner had Toby wondered what that action might be than the answer came through as clear as a bell. His uncle had told him to work harder "to catch the Christmas spirit." That was it!

Toby could feel himself really getting excited now. Enough of the puzzle pieces were in place that he was beginning to see the entire picture. The more he thought about it, the more the idea of the Christmas book being magical made sense. There was only one thing to do. He would put it to the test.

That afternoon, he left his office a couple of hours early "to catch the Christmas spirit." He had thought about it all day and concluded that such soul enrichment required the performance of some charitable act. He began his quest by emptying all of his pocket change into the bucket of the first bell-ringing charity Santa Claus that he came across. Then, he gave a five dollar bill to a man holding a piece of cardboard with "Hungry. Please Help" written on it. Next, Toby went into a discount toy store and bought trucks, dolls, building blocks, and coloring books, delivering them all to the family shelter near his office. Finally, he made out a check to his church's charity fund and delivered it to the minister on his way home.

Toby felt quite content with himself and quite filled with the Christmas spirit as he settled into the den that night. His plate was piled extra high with butter cookies, and he hadn't made any effort to spare the whipped cream on top of the hot chocolate. He looked upon the leather-bound book with renewed admiration instead of a frown. Tonight, he was sure the stories would be well worth reading.

The next story seemed particularly fitting, since it involved a Christmas tree adorned with magical ornaments: ornaments upon which the writing and the painted figures changed, telling of neighbors that needed help and advising of good deeds to be done. The family upon whose tree the ornaments hung believed in their magic and were making a wonderful Christmas of bringing good cheer everywhere the ornaments directed them.

Toby's spirit soared as he read the tale. Things were going just fine in this story, and he was sure that he understood why. He had given of himself and was now reaping the blessings of that labor. Things were going fine, that is, until Toby got to the final paragraph. With absolutely no warning or apparent cause, the ornaments all fell from the tree, shattering into a million pieces, and the husband discovered that his business partner had been cheating him, having embezzled all of the family's life savings.

"The End"

Toby was crushed. This was the most ludicrous ending yet. What had he done wrong? Toby went to bed with a stomachache that night, having consumed the entire plate of butter cookies out of sheer frustration and discouragement.

Unable to sleep, he thought about calling his uncle

again but decided against it. Uncle Wayne would probably just tell him to try harder. Toby looked over at his wife, peacefully sleeping. He resisted the impulse to waken her and unload his frustrations.

The next morning, as Toby reflected on his charitable efforts of the previous day, he decided that maybe he was going about it all wrong. Maybe giving away money and buying a few things just wasn't enough. Perhaps he needed to give more of his time to others. He couldn't just take off work again, so he laid out a plan of attack for the next several nights.

Of course, the first people he thought of were his wife and children. Tonight, he wouldn't tuck himself away in the den but instead would spend the entire evening with those he loved most. He would help his wife with whatever she happened to be doing and would read to the kids or help them put up more Christmas decorations.

Then, he thought of his mother and of their last phone conversation. The whole family would visit her on Christmas Day, but Toby had promised that he would visit her before then. He would reserve tomorrow night to make good that promise. As he thought about the upcoming visit, a knot began to form in his stomach. What if she was still talking about going home? He really didn't want to get into that with her. There was no way she could live alone. He pictured her living with his family, and the knot in his stomach grew even bigger. It just wouldn't work; he knew that. But it was when he tried listing specific reasons why it wouldn't work that he ran into trouble. The house was big enough. The kids would love having their grandmother close by. Lindsay, his wife, had made it clear that if the need ever arose, his mother was welcome to live with them. But she had never pushed the idea, knowing that Toby would have to feel the same way or the arrangement would never work. And now came the hard part. Toby had to admit to himself that, for whatever reason, he didn't feel the same way. He got along with his mother on short visits. But living together? If he were honest, he'd have to admit that it was simply more of an inconvenient change of lifestyle than he was willing to endure. Besides, he thought, the need for such a change really hadn't arisen. The care his mother was receiving at Rosewood was top notch. She'd be fine. Everyone her age had to deal with a little more loneliness than they wanted to, he reasoned. In any event, this wasn't something that had to be decided right away. There was no urgency. Nothing had to change right now. He would go and have a nice visit with his mother tomorrow evening, and that would be a good thing. Resolved that such a course of action was proper and sufficient for the time being, Toby shifted his attention to the stack of papers on his desk.

As the day wore on, Toby's thoughts wandered to other ways in which he could be of service to even more people. It made sense that he extend his circle of care, going beyond his wife and children. A lot of possibilities came to mind, but none of them seemed to have any special appeal. He went over the short list he had generated again and again. Finally, a new idea came to mind, one that suited his purposes perfectly and would be a lot of fun.

After work, Toby raced to his car and headed to the mall. An hour later he emerged, his arms filled with packages. His purchases included a Santa suit, complete with beard, spectacles, and black boots, boxes of candy canes, holiday stickers, a ring of sleigh bells, and a childrens' Christmas story book. He made sure that there wasn't anything tricky about the book, and that it had a happy ending. He practiced "Ho-ho-ho"ing all the way home. Toby pictured himself making cheer-filled visits to children in the local hospital, to family shelters, to friends' homes, and to a sheltered workshop. He was looking forward to these visits, but tonight would be devoted entirely to his family.

The evening went wonderfully. He spent more time with his children than he had in quite awhile. They laughed and talked and made a gigantic red and green paper chain. Later that evening, they secretly decorated a neighbor's yard with the chain. Toby decided not to try reading any of the stories in the leather bound volume that night. He would wait until tomorrow night, or maybe even a couple more nights, depending on how many Santa Claus visits he made.

Late the next afternoon, Toby made good on his promise to visit his mother. She looked better. Her eyes were bright, there was a fresh glow on her cheeks, and she was glad to see her son. She spoke enthusiastically of going home and shared her holiday gift giving plans with him. How could she be so unrealistic? Toby listened superficially, occasionally nodding, smiling, or giving a one-line reply to her questions. His attention was really focused on his own thoughts, wrapped in his own holiday plans. As he left, his mother reminded him of his promise to bring the entire family on Christmas Day.

The two nights following his visit to his mother convinced Toby that his Santa routine would have to become an annual event. The agencies he contacted were delighted to have him come, and the reception he received at each stop couldn't have been better. Surprise, excitement and gratitude unfolded in a flurry of "ho-ho-ho's"; jingling bells; Christmas carols; candy canes; reindeer and snowman stickers on hands, cheeks, and foreheads; the reading of a delightful Christmas story; and the inevitable lists for Santa. He decided that next year he might bring an elf or two along to help out.

The surprise visits to his friends' homes were just as delightful. The children squealed with glee when Santa would sit their dad on his lap and give him a lecture on how he needed to be better or he wasn't going to get anything but a lump of coal in his Christmas stocking. Leaving a few bewildered friends and neighbors in his wake, Toby "Claus" covered a lot of territory those two nights.

Entering his den at the end of the fourth night, Toby thought back on how he had tried to capture the "pure essence of Christmas" tucked away by himself in this little room. He now realized that he had been very mistaken. His recent labors had made it quite clear that the light of Christmas burns brightest when one gives of oneself to others. With a quiet confidence, he picked up the book, re-reading the now familiar title, "A Christmas Especially for You." Tonight he would read the last remaining story. Perhaps now the ending would change and the stories truly would be for him. He turned the pages slowly until he found his place. He began reading of a little old woman who lived alone. It was a time of war, and her son was spending the Christmas season in the trenches of a battlefield far from home . . . .

Gifts meant nothing to the woman. What she longed for more than anything else in the world was word from her son letting her know that he was safe. He had written her regularly in the many months he had been gone, but far too many weeks had passed since she'd received his last letter. A note, even if it was just a single sentence, would bring her the greatest of Christmas joy.

Now, it was Christmas Eve, and she wrapped her shawl tightly about her shoulders as she made her way slowly to the mail box. Undoing the latch, her fingers shaking with anticipation, she lowered the door. The box was empty.

The End

Toby closed his eyes and let his head fall against the back of the chair. He frowned and his lips were pursed tightly together. The disappointment was almost overwhelming. He didn't rant and rave as he had on nights past. The hurt was much deeper tonight. He thought back on all the effort he had put into the last few days.

After several minutes, he raised his head and looked again at the book. He closed the cover, regretting that he had read the last remaining story. It was finished, and there was nothing more to hope for. All of the tales had been read; all of the endings were known. He resolved that he would never again open the book.

As he thought about it, the ridiculous stories in this ridiculous volume just didn't matter all that much. He knew how good he had felt, giving of himself these past few days. And he knew how bad he felt when he had anything to do with this miserable book. That said it all.

The fact that his uncle had vowed that each story truly did have a happy ending didn't matter now. The fact that he'd been promised that he could come to know those endings was of little importance to him. Toby knew what it took to make the Christmas spirit flourish in his heart, and it had nothing to do with a bunch of story endings. His uncle had been wrong when he'd foretold that the happy endings would change his Christmases forever. This Christmas had already changed for Toby, and it was a change for the better: a change that he would incorporate into every Christmas for the rest of his life. And so, the book would be closed, never to be opened again.

The next day, Toby was miserable. In spite of his resolve, and no matter how hard he tried, Toby could not keep his thoughts from returning to the last story he had read: a mother praying for her son's safety, and yearning for some contact with him, even if only through two or three lines penned weeks earlier. Toby's imagination took over, and he pictured himself, decked out in his Santa suit, briskly walking up the path to the old woman's cottage and knocking at her door. She would open the door only a few inches, being a bit startled at the white-bearded stranger dressed all in red. But she would be unable to resist his smiling eyes (Toby truly believed he had this effect on all women!) and would open the door a little further. He would wish her a Merry Christmas and would hand her the long-awaited letter from her son. As her eyes filled with tears and she brought her hand to her mouth in utter amazement, Toby would tell her that he had just come from seeing her son and that he was safe and well.

As he wiped the tears from his own eyes, Toby decided that he did a lot better job of creating story endings than the goof who had originally written the book. Suddenly, uninvited thoughts of his own mother filled his mind, and Toby cringed as pangs of guilt rushed through him. How willing he had been to bring joy to an imaginary mother with an imaginary son. He sat in silence for quite some time.

The thought came to him that giving came in many sizes and shapes. There was the kind of giving that took but a few minutes, a few hours, or, at most, a few days. And then there was a deeper, richer kind of giving: recompense for that which had been given so freely by another over so many years, even over a lifetime. There was one more story ending to be written, Toby pondered, and this one had to be written by him.

❄ ❄ ❄

Agnes Whitaker looked up to see what all the commotion was about. She thought she recognized the people entering the day room of the convalescent center, but she couldn't be sure without putting her glasses on. With her bifocals in place, she focused on the figures crossing the room toward her. She was right. It was three of her grandchildren and her daughter-in-law, and they had a terribly scrawny Santa Claus with them. Concentrating on the eyes and on what little of the face she could see behind the pitiful beard, she wrinkled her brow.

"Toby, is that you in there? What in the world are you doing?"

"Don't you believe in Santa Claus?" her son asked in the deepest voice he could muster.

Looking down at the floor, she pursed her lips tightly and struggled to hide her disappointment. The fact that the entire family was paying her this early visit could mean only one thing. There had been a change of plans, and they wouldn't be coming to see her on Christmas Day.

Her gaze fixed on the tile floor, she tried desperately to think of something cheerful to say. Her attention was drawn back to her family when Toby placed a small box in her lap. It was about three inches square, wrapped in bright green paper and topped with a shiny gold bow. Agnes hated herself for having such thoughts, but she couldn't help thinking that the tiny box, no matter what it contained, just wasn't much of a consolation prize for not getting to spend Christmas Day with her family.

Nevertheless, she said something or other, trying to sound surprised and enthused. Although her heart wasn't in it, she unwrapped the miniature package and took off the lid. Removing the cotton square that covered the box's contents, she was speechless, not because the present was so wonderful, but because she simply didn't understand. There, on a second pad of cotton, lay a plain, ordinary key. Looking at each of the five faces staring down at her, she found they were all smiling. Nobody said a word; they just smiled.

Toby knelt down at the side of his mother's chair, taking her hand in his. "Mom, the very best Christmas present we could get this year would be for you to come and stay with us."

His mother nodded her head and answered, "Well, that would be quite nice, to spend the day at your place."

Toby interrupted her, "Mom, we don't just mean for Christmas Day. We mean we want you to came and live with us, all the time." Pointing to the box, Toby added, "That's what the key is for. It's a key to the front door of our house — your house."

Toby's mother looked at her daughter-in-law, and Lindsay nodded her approval. "Please say yes, Mom. We'd love to have you live with us," Lindsay added.

"Are you sure?" Agnes asked, looking her son in the eyes.

"I'm positive, Mom," Toby whispered.

The children chimed in with a chorus of "me too!"s, and everybody was hugging everybody.

The next day Toby's house was filled with a flurry of activity. Boxes, clothing, and furniture were moved. A bedroom and bath were prepared. That evening, Toby lay stretched out on the family room floor watching the crackling blaze in the fireplace. There had been no time to worry about story endings, but Toby was avoiding the den, still intent on his abandonment of the Christmas book.

"Oh, what a wonderful little Christmas story!" Toby's mother exclaimed. He didn't know how long she'd been sitting behind him on the couch, but her enthusiastic remark caused him to turn.

"What did you say, Mom?" he asked, giving her a casual glance and then rolling back to face the fire. But his head snapped back around, when it finally registered exactly what she was holding. Toby's mother had the Christmas book in her lap. No mistake about it. Dark leather cover with "A Christmas Especially for You" emblazoned on it in decorative gold lettering.

Looking up at her son, she explained, "That man at the Christmas tree lot was so sweet to secretly follow the little boy home and then come back with a tree and presents for his family."

Toby panicked, thinking that perhaps his mother's condition had been more frail than he'd thought. Maybe the excitement of coming to live with them was proving too much for her. But then again . . . .

His mother let out a shriek as Toby leaped from the floor and landed on the couch next to her. Acting in a manner she considered to be quite rude, her son snatched the book from her lap and silently read the last page of the story. And then he slowly read it out loud, pointing to each word, much as he had when he was first learning to read. For the longest time, Toby just sat there, staring at the words: *"The End."*

Sure enough, the story ending had changed. The printing on the page was definitely different from what it had been the first night he had read the book. No more snapping the lock shut and going off to his own Christmas celebration. Instead, a kind-hearted Christmas tree vendor was secretly leaving not only a Christmas tree, but a load of food and presents on the doorstep of the little boy's home.

Taking her son by the arm, Toby's mother anxiously questioned: "Toby, what in the world is the matter?"

Without looking up, Toby simply pointed at the page; "This story has a happy ending."

Peering at her son over the top of her bifocals, she studied him carefully. Perhaps he'd become quite frail. Maybe the excitement of having her move in with the family was proving too much for him. In a soothing tone, she replied, "Yes, I thought so too. Isn't that nice."

Glancing at his mother out of the corner of his eye, Toby realized he was being pacified. He also realized that there was absolutely no way he was going to be able to explain this bizarre business — at least not right now. He tried to slip out of the awkward corner he'd placed himself in by offering, "I think I must be confusing this story with another one I read. You know how many stories you can go through in a Christmas season." He wasn't sure how convincing his performance had been, but it appeared his mother wasn't going to pursue the matter.

Directing his attention back to the book, Toby began turning pages rapidly. The ending to each and every story had changed. Emilia Quigley was delighted that her father had consented to her marrying Jacob T. Dawson. The name of Arthur Bobbington had vanished into thin air. The little girl who had dreamed of the one special dolly all year long found her under the tree on Christmas morning. The boy who'd saved all his money to buy his mother just the right gift walked past the storm drain without incident, went into the store and bought his mother's present. Toby was particularly glad to find that a truce had been declared, and the old woman's son was able to come home for Christmas. And, turning to the final story, he discovered that the polar bear had safely guided the lost elves back to the North Pole in plenty of time to load Santa's sleigh. As wonderful as these endings were, they were still upsetting. This would take awhile to think through.

Over the next couple of days, the pieces slowly began to fall into place. Toby realized that his efforts at giving a little money, or at doing something that he enjoyed, like playing Santa Claus, hadn't been enough to change the stories. He remembered his uncle's warning that the stories "may not be as easily finished as you think." That had been followed by admonitions to "persist" and to "Do what you must to finish the book. It will be well worth the effort."

Toby understood that it was only after he had gotten past doing the things that were convenient and easy and had done something that really required him to give of himself that the stories had changed. He remembered that each time he'd spoken with Uncle Wayne about the book, the conversation had always turned to questions about Toby's mother. He was rather embarrassed that having his own mother come and live with them qualified as something that had been hard for him to do. But, the important thing was that he had done what was right.

On Christmas morning, Toby watched the joy that filled his mother's face and his children's faces as they laughed and chatted and had a wonderful time together. He realized that his uncle had been right. Nothing short